If she was ri...
their lives, and the third...

"I wish I could say these other trails are dogworthy, but it's been nearly two years since the women were on these trails," he said and gathered up the photos of those areas, but as he did so, he noticed another set of pictures in her file.

He reached for them, but she stayed his hand with hers. He noticed her hand tremble as she did so and heard her say in a soft tone, "That one's not pertinent right now."

She shot to her feet, marched to her murder board and rapped her knuckles against its surface. "The clock is ticking, and I worry that once he murders her, we'll lose his trail until he takes another victim."

Her gaze gleamed with determination but also that sadness he had seen earlier that day. He understood the determination. As for the sadness, he hoped he'd one day understand what had put it there.

COLD CASE K-9

CARIDAD PIÑEIRO

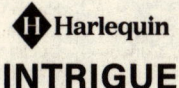

INTRIGUE

If you purchased this book without a cover you should be aware that this book is stolen property. It was reported as "unsold and destroyed" to the publisher, and neither the author nor the publisher has received any payment for this "stripped book."

MIX
Paper | Supporting responsible forestry
FSC® C021394

Harlequin® INTRIGUE™

Recycling programs for this product may not exist in your area.

ISBN-13: 978-1-335-69038-8

Cold Case K-9

Copyright © 2025 by Caridad Piñeiro Scordato

All rights reserved. No part of this book may be used or reproduced in any manner whatsoever without written permission.

Without limiting the exclusive rights of any author, contributor or the publisher of this publication, any unauthorized use of this publication to train generative artificial intelligence (AI) technologies is expressly prohibited. Harlequin also exercises their rights under Article 4(3) of the Digital Single Market Directive 2019/790 and expressly reserves this publication from the text and data mining exception.

This is a work of fiction. Names, characters, places and incidents are either the product of the author's imagination or are used fictitiously. Any resemblance to actual persons, living or dead, businesses, companies, events or locales is entirely coincidental.

For questions and comments about the quality of this book, please contact us at CustomerService@Harlequin.com.

TM and ® are trademarks of Harlequin Enterprises ULC.

Harlequin Enterprises ULC
22 Adelaide St. West, 41st Floor
Toronto, Ontario M5H 4E3, Canada
www.Harlequin.com

HarperCollins Publishers
Macken House, 39/40 Mayor Street Upper,
Dublin 1, D01 C9W8, Ireland
www.HarperCollins.com

Printed in Lithuania

New York Times and *USA TODAY* bestselling author **Caridad Piñeiro** is a Jersey girl who just wants to write and is the author of nearly fifty novels and novellas. She loves romance novels, superheroes, TV and cooking. For more information on Caridad and her dark, sexy romantic suspense and paranormal romances, please visit www.caridad.com.

Books by Caridad Piñeiro

Harlequin Intrigue

Crooked Pass Security

Cliffside Kidnapping
Defended by the Bodyguard
Cold Case K-9

South Beach Security: K-9 Division

Sabotage Operation
Escape the Everglades
Killer in the Kennel
Danger in Dade

South Beach Security

Lost in Little Havana
Brickell Avenue Ambush
Biscayne Bay Breach

Cold Case Reopened
Trapping a Terrorist
Decoy Training

Visit the Author Profile page at Harlequin.com.

CAST OF CHARACTERS

Diego Rodriguez—Diego Rodriguez is a trained K-9 handler who has worked as a military policeman as well as in local law enforcement. He is a new agent with Crooked Pass Security and will help them with investigations as well as the creation of a new K-9 division in Colorado.

Gabriella Ruiz—Gabriella Ruiz was sixteen when her twelve-year-old sister, Isabella, was taken from a Girl Scout camping trip and was never found. Isabella's disappearance drove Gabriella to go into law enforcement, where she is now an agent for the Colorado Bureau of Investigation.

Poppy—This five-year-old German Shepherd is a trained cadaver dog who has also been recently trained to do search and rescue.

Robert (Robbie) Whitaker—Robbie Whitaker is a computer genius who works closely with his younger sister, Sophie, at the newly formed Crooked Pass Security, a branch of South Beach Security that helps solve crimes and protect vulnerable people.

Ryder Hunt—Ryder Hunt works for the Colorado Bureau of Investigation. A former Marine who served in Afghanistan, Ryder has been asked by Gabriella Ruiz to partner with him to find a missing hiker and investigate whether her disappearance is linked to a possible serial killer.

Josefina (Sophie) Whitaker—Sophie Whitaker is a computer genius who is working with her brother at Crooked Pass Security. An MIT graduate, she and her older brother, Robbie, had started a business together in Silicon Beach before joining South Beach Security with their Gonzalez cousins in Miami.

Prologue

The early spring sun bathed her face as she stood on the mountain trail. She walked to the lip and peered down a nearby ravine to the creek at its base. Along the edges of the crystal-clear water, spring was coming alive with the first hints of green and purple. Before long, those little slips of color would unfurl into mountain bluebells and the tall, hairy leaves of cow parsnip.

In the trees nearby, bright green buds were bursting open as life returned to the Colorado mountains.

She loved this time of year that held so much promise.

Shielding her eyes against the sun, she glanced up the trail, reviewing how much farther she had to go before reaching the summit.

Not far, she thought, but the day was still early, and she didn't want to rush her hike. She wanted to savor the day. Tomorrow she'd be trapped behind walls of glass and cement while at work.

Walking to the other side of the trail, a challenging one for more experienced hikers, she sat on a boulder warmed by the sun and laid her knapsack at her feet. Rummaging through it, she hauled out a baggie with trail mix to satisfy the hunger in her belly.

The snap of a branch behind her snared her attention.

Something dark and menacing charged at her before she could react.

Peanuts, chocolate and raisins went flying as she was slammed onto the ground.

The force of the impact drove her breath from her. Before she could take another breath, a gloved hand covered her mouth.

She fought for breath and freedom, but he was just too heavy. Too big. Too strong.

Circles of black whirled before her eyes. In her mind, a silent scream rang out.

I don't want to die.

As the blackness thickened, taking her away, that small desperate voice pleaded.

Please, I don't want to die.

Chapter One

"I'm really sorry we have to do this, Diego. My hands are tied on account of what happened with the senator," said Police Chief Jackson Whitaker.

"I understand, Jax," Diego Rodriguez replied. Ever since the senator had been arrested for crimes including alleged rape, money laundering and kidnapping, any project in which the senator had been involved was being reviewed and reassessed.

"I feel bad. You just relocated for this gig," Jackson said. "If you're not sure about making that rental permanent, you're welcome to stay with Rhea and me until this is all cleared up."

Diego appreciated the offer, but since his friend had a new baby, he didn't want to intrude. Waving off the invitation, he said, "I appreciate it, but I'm sure I can get a job as a security guard or something until everything is straightened out."

"Actually, I thought this might interest you," Jackson said, and passed a business card to Diego.

Crooked Pass Security. The company had a Denver address and indicated that it was a branch of South Beach Security. He'd worked with SBS before when Jackson had been investigating the disappearance of his wife's twin sister and more recently, during the kidnapping case involving State Senator Oliver.

Diego held the card up. "I don't get it. What's SBS doing here?"

"SBS tech geniuses Sophie and Robbie Whitaker helped us

with the Oliver case, and they've decided to put down roots in Colorado," Jackson explained.

Not strange considering Sophie and Robbie were Jackson's cousins and visited regularly. Plus, he'd heard that the two had found love with the people who'd helped them during the investigations. Robbie was involved with Jax's sister-in-law Selene while his sister Sophie had fallen for CBI Agent Ryder Hunt.

"What does this have to do with me?" Diego asked, and tried to return the business card to Jackson, but his friend urged him to keep it.

"They need good investigators and are also hoping to build a K-9 division here. I think you'd be a perfect fit."

Diego examined the card again. From what he knew of the SBS agency and the brother-and-sister tech experts who had been such a help during recent investigations, they were bright, hardworking, successful and friendly. He did not doubt they'd treat anyone who worked for them well.

As he met Jackson's gaze across the width of the heavy old oak desk in his office, he finally realized that it might be some time before Jackson would be able to allow him and his K-9, Poppy, onto the police force again.

Slipping the card into the pocket of his shirt uniform, he said, "Thanks for this. I'll check it out."

GABRIELLA RUIZ LAID the reports and photos with details of a missing hiker on her desk. The young woman had disappeared the day before, and the local police department had reached out to the Colorado Bureau of Investigation for help.

She diligently reviewed the information, flagging details that might be helpful. It was impossible not to notice the similarities to two other cases that she could not forget. Women who had also gone out for just a day of fresh air and sunshine only to disappear.

Just like her sister had disappeared, she thought.

Standing, she grabbed a photo of the missing woman, Jeannie Roberts, and walked over to the murder board she had on one wall of her office. She tacked Jeannie's photo beside those of the two missing women. All twentysomething brunettes. All beautiful. All avid hikers and athletes much like Gabriella herself.

And much like her sister Isabella, except she'd only been twelve when she'd gone missing.

A few taps on the frame of her door drew her attention.

"Heard you caught the Roberts case," said her colleague Ryder Hunt as he sauntered into her office.

"I did. I need a partner on this one. You interested?" she said, and gestured for him to take a seat.

His gaze drifted from her to the board and then back to her. "Depends," he almost drawled.

She arched a dark brow. "On what?"

He gestured to the board. "You still trying to connect those two cold cases? And now this one?"

Gabriella did a slow turn and scrutinized the board, wanting to be certain of the answer she gave her friend and colleague. With a decisive nod, she faced Ryder and said, "I am."

His eyes opened slightly wider. "Because of Isabella?"

She couldn't deny that every case like this brought reminders of her sister. It was the reason she'd decided to go into law enforcement. Isabella had never received justice, and her family had never gotten closure. She wanted to keep other families from a similar fate.

Unfazed by her colleague's obvious worry, she said, "Yes. For Isabella and these women. Someone has to figure out what happened to them."

Ryder did that slow perusal again. Her. The board. Her, before he finally said, "These disappearances happened over six months apart and it's been what, two years since they took place?"

"Numerous serial killers—"

"Whoa, that's a big leap. Plus, those are only two," Ryder shot out.

Gabriella pointed at the board. "In 2008, the FBI defined serial murder to be the unlawful killing of *two* or more victims."

The flush of angry color swept across Ryder's cheeks as with a slow dip of his head, he said, "I know, Gabby. You don't have to quote scripture to me."

Gabriella muttered a curse beneath her breath and shook her head in apology. "I'm sorry, Ryder. I'm just so…" She hesitated, searching for the right word, and finally gave up and said, "Determined. I'm determined to find out where they are. What happened."

"That kind of determination can lead you to lose focus," Ryder reminded.

Ryder wasn't wrong. "Which is why it's even more important to have a good partner to keep me in line."

Ryder hesitated but then dipped his head in agreement. "If the chief agrees, you've got your partner."

Chapter Two

I love watching them wake up.

I love that look that joyfully says, I'm alive.

I love seeing that joy fade as reality registers and fear sets in.

He wished he could experience those looks again and again as the days passed. But he couldn't hold on to her for too long even with all the precautions he'd taken.

The root cellar in the cabin was soundproof, protection against any screams alerting distant neighbors or hikers to what was happening.

He'd learned that the hard way many years earlier when he'd had a screamer. Even though he was a good distance away from any real civilization, he'd worried someone might have heard and come to spoil his pleasure.

That night's fear of discovery had morphed into disappointment at having to get rid of his toy earlier than planned.

But not this time, he thought as he eased on the black hood, grabbed his camera and slipped down the stairs. At the base of the steps, he flipped a switch and bright stage lights snapped to life.

She shot awake, eyes opened as wide as a deer in the headlights. Pulling up her knees, she wrapped her arms around them to hide her naked body from his gaze. In a tiny voice, she said, "Please. Please don't hurt me again."

Pleasure filled him at her fear. "You know what to do," he said. At her hesitation, he reached for the large bowie knife at his side and held it up so that the light from the powerful spotlights made the sharp edge glint with menace.

Her breathing raced and her body trembled, but she slowly opened her arms and legs wide. The metal shackles on her wrists and ankles rasped against the cement floor of the cellar with her movement.

He sheathed the knife and took the photo. The click of the shutter was loud in the otherwise silent room.

At the second click of the shutter, she turned her face, averting her gaze.

"Look at me," he said, and was about to reach for the knife again, but she instantly complied.

It disappointed him that she had been complacent so far. He liked his women with a little more fight, and she'd been like a cold, dead fish as he'd satisfied himself with her the day before.

"You're weak. Stupid," he challenged, hoping for some spirit, and it finally blossomed.

Her back straightened slightly, and her eyes narrowed, fear fleeing as strength flooded into her. "I'm going to get out of this and when I do..." Her voice trailed off as he snapped another photo, wanting to capture that spirit forever.

"What are you going to do?" he goaded, wanting the dangerous animal everyone had inside them to emerge.

"I'm going to kill you," she said, her voice deadly cold. Fire blazing in her eyes.

He laughed, snapped another photo and then laid the camera on the nearby table. Easing the knife from the sheath on his belt, he held it up again.

"Not if I kill you first."

DIEGO SAT ACROSS the conference room table from Sophie and Robbie Whitaker, the South Beach Security tech geniuses who had decided to stay with the Colorado branch of the family and form Crooked Pass Security.

"We're just getting started so it's a little slow, but we're optimistic things will pick up soon," Sophie said, twined her fingers together and laid them on the leather portfolio before her.

"Where do I fit in?" Diego asked, wondering how a company that had just opened and had little or no work could afford to take on more personnel.

"We sometimes need K-9 handlers in addition to smart investigators. You fill both those slots," Robbie said, and shot a glance at Sophie before he passed a set of papers across the table.

An employment contract, Diego realized as he picked up the papers. His eyes almost bugged out at the salary they were offering. Nearly twice what he'd been getting paid at the Regina Police Department.

"You know the old saying, if it's too good to be true," he said as he skimmed a finger down the terms in the contract. But the terms all seemed reasonable.

"We have the backing of the Miami cousins and luckily, both Robbie and I are financially secure, if that's what you're worried about," Sophie explained.

That was part of it, Diego thought. The other part was that he didn't want to leave Jackson in a lurch if his town council found that there hadn't been any wrongdoing thanks to the senator's involvement with the new police hires. But the salary they were proposing would let him be financially secure and maybe even have enough left over to help other veterans rebuild their lives.

Peering across the table at the siblings, he said, "When do I start?"

RYDER AND GABRIELLA had reviewed all the reports on the hiker's disappearance. But as far as she was concerned, nothing was better than a real-life visit to the scene. Plus, there was the added benefit that it was a glorious spring day.

She sucked in a deep breath and imagined how the hiker must

have felt the day she disappeared. The weather had been much like it was today, Gabriella thought as she and Ryder trudged up the trail they had identified as the one where Jeannie Roberts had disappeared. Her car had been found at the trailhead after she'd been reported missing by her partner.

A partner who was still a person of interest until they could eliminate him as a suspect.

But first Gabriella wanted to get a sense of the crime scene and the other information they'd gleaned from the police reports.

They were halfway up the trail, one usually only traveled by more experienced hikers, when they reached the spot where Roberts had allegedly been taken. Police tape marked off an area and as Gabriella examined it, she concurred that this had likely been the spot.

The ground showed signs of a disturbance. There were some nuts and raisins on the ground that local animals and birds hadn't yet scavenged. A nearby boulder provided a perfect place to sit and view the beauty of the landscape.

"She stopped to enjoy the day and get some fuel before she continued to the summit," Gabriella said, and pointed up the trail with the tip of her hiking pole.

Ryder shielded his eyes against the sun, examined the trail and nodded. "Sure looks that way."

Gabriella did a slow pivot and perused the area around them. On the far side of the trail was a drop-off to the ravine below where a mountain creek flowed at its center. A forest of pines and aspens lined the other side of the trail.

With a shake of her head, she said, "How did he get her down the trail without being noticed?"

Ryder mimicked her action, scrutinizing the scene before he pursed his lips and blew out an exasperated sigh. "Slow day on the trail maybe, but he'd have to be strong to carry her out," he said, and gestured with his pole to the difficult path they had taken.

"Maybe he didn't carry her. If he subdued her and had a weapon—"

"She hiked back down with him. Even if they'd met someone on the trek back, they might not have noticed anything was out of the ordinary," Gabriella finished for him and then pushed on. "Roberts has been gone nearly thirty-six hours now. Every hour that goes by is an hour closer to her death."

Ryder met her gaze. "We've got every possible person working this case, but I know some people who might see something new and also help us with those cold cases you want to reopen."

"The chief nixed spending any time or funds on those older cases," Gabriella reminded.

Ryder grinned and used air quotes as he replied, "He said we couldn't spend any time 'on the clock' and don't worry about the cost. My friends love a challenge."

"Really? Who would they be?" Gabriella asked as she started back down to the trailhead. She was eager to return to the office and run through all the information they had so far to see if anything could help them save the missing hiker.

"Crooked Pass Security. They've got connections and capabilities that you wouldn't believe. Are you game?"

Was she game to locate Jeannie Roberts and find out who had killed the other two women? Maybe even finally know what had happened to her sister Isabella?

"I'm game."

Her photo was plastered across every local newspaper, television station and social media.

It didn't worry him. No one had seen them hike down that day. He'd done well by choosing that trail since it was a harder hike that few people would do, especially that early in the season when there might still be traces of ice and snow at the higher elevations of the summit because of last week's unseasonable snow.

He'd done well this time, unlike some of his experiences with earlier women. He'd started by taking them in their homes, but he hadn't liked it as much. The fast kills hadn't given him time to enjoy their fear and their bodies.

That's when he'd decided to use the trails to take his victims.

At first, he'd worried that people had seen him hiking with his victims and that someone might connect the two incidents and identify him, but it hadn't happened.

And much like he'd learned about the screams, he'd learned to be more careful and to hide his face beneath a baseball cap, mask or neck gaiter.

Finally, thanks to various television shows and news articles, he'd known what to do to not leave any DNA behind after the first one.

Well, not really the first one. The first one had happened nearly five years earlier.

He'd been a teen then. Young and inexperienced. He hadn't even meant to kill her. He'd just wanted to have some fun. Explore some of what he'd seen online and in the magazines his father kept hidden in his office desk.

I didn't mean to kill her, he thought again, but admitted to himself that once it had happened, he'd liked it. A lot.

So much so that he'd kept her around for nearly a week before panic and the smell had begun to set in and he knew he had to get rid of the young girl's body.

He still visited her every now and again. Firsts were always special, and it thrilled him that they'd yet to find her. He didn't think they ever would. Or the others either. They were buried close by so that he wouldn't have far to go when he visited.

He'd hidden them well, he thought as need rose in him, so strongly that he couldn't just sit at his desk anymore, looking at sheets with numbers that meant little.

Jumping to his feet, he slipped on his jacket, straightened his tie and hurried out of his office.

The receptionist at the front desk smiled as he pushed through the doors. "Have a nice night," she called out.

He smiled and did a friendly wave. "I plan to do just that."

Chapter Three

Diego prowled the conference room restlessly, his German shepherd K-9, Poppy, at his side. He'd spent his first two days at Crooked Pass Security in meetings with the family members who ran South Beach Security, the main branch of the company.

He had been impressed by the Miami cousins, whose grandfather and father had built the agency and turned it over to the next generation to run. He'd also been surprised with what they could bring to investigations, from a brand-new K-9 training facility to incredible technology thanks to the marriage of one of the cousins to John Wilson, a well-known tech billionaire with an innovative program and seemingly endless capabilities.

But Diego wasn't used to sitting in meetings, which was why he was now pacing back and forth in the conference room, waiting for yet another meeting. But at least this one was about an investigation, and he looked forward to helping in any way he could.

As the door to the conference room opened, Diego whirled to face it.

Sophie and Robbie Whitaker entered, followed by a handsome dark-haired man he recognized from the case he'd worked on a few weeks earlier involving the kidnapping of Sophie and Robbie's parents.

A second later, a woman entered. But she wasn't just any woman.

Dark, nearly black hair drifted down against the bright white of her shirt and the lapels of her serious navy-blue pantsuit. Her eyes were just as dark, bottomless almost, as her gaze locked with his.

Something passed between them, and it tugged at his heart more than his gut.

She'd known loss.

He didn't know how he knew it, but he did, and it awoke a similar emotion in him.

But as quickly as that connection came, it evaporated as her shields went up.

Sophie, ever-observant Sophie, must have caught the moment, since she held her hand out in the direction of the woman and man who had entered and said, "Diego. I believe you know CBI Agent Ryder Hunt already. This is his partner, CBI Agent Gabriella Ruiz."

Gabriella. A beautiful name for a beautiful woman, he thought, and as he shook her hand, that feeling of connection swept through him again.

"Nice to meet you, Agent Ruiz," Diego said, and reluctantly released her hand.

"Likewise, Agent Rodriguez," Gabriella said, and was instantly all business as she faced Sophie and Robbie. "I know Ryder has already sent over the information."

Sophie nodded and gestured for them to sit. Once they were all settled, him with Poppy at his feet, he sat back as Gabriella reviewed the materials.

Gabriella displayed information from her laptop on a large television on the far wall of the conference room.

"I came across these cold cases about a year ago during a regular review, and I couldn't forget them," she said, and brought up photos of two women along with pertinent info.

"Missy Cornerstone and Alyssa Nations were twenty-two and twenty-four, respectively, when they were taken. Both Caucasian. Both attended the University of Denver, likely at the same time."

"Lots of similarities. Do you think whoever took them might have been there also?" Robbie jumped in to ask.

"Possibly. Files show that local police and CBI spoke to their boyfriends as well as several persons of interest. But they did not find any overlap between the two cases," Ryder advised.

Lots of similarities but also differences, Diego thought as he skimmed through the copies of the files Gabriella and Ryder had provided. "The women were taken from hiking trails but at different times of the year," he said, and gestured to the television where the photos of the two women almost screamed at them.

Look for me! Look for me!

"They have very similar features," he added as he perused the photos and then slipped a snapshot of the missing hiker from the papers. He held it up and said, "Just like Jeannie Roberts."

"Just like her, which is why I think all three of these cases are connected," Gabriella said with a nod and tight smile.

Diego couldn't argue, but he also couldn't wholeheartedly agree. "It's been two years since these other women disappeared. Plus, there's what…a gap of six months in between these two older abductions."

"BTK had cooling-off periods of as much as ten years between killings. The Grim Sleeper had one gap of almost fourteen years between murders," Gabriella advised.

"Are you saying you suspect a serial killer took Jeannie Roberts?" Sophie asked as she, too, flipped through her copy of the files.

GABRIELLA SHARED A long look with Ryder, aware that he wasn't necessarily on board with her designation of the cases.

"I believe so, but Ryder isn't as sure as I am," she admitted, wanting full disclosure with the team that might help them.

"I'm no expert on serial killers, but aren't they rare?" Diego asked, his gaze fixed on her intently.

His eyes were a deep brown, open and welcoming. When their gazes had locked earlier, she'd felt that welcome and something more. Something she couldn't define, which bothered her, so she dragged her gaze away, nodded and explained. "Less than 1 percent of all murders in the US are connected to serial killers, but the FBI estimates that there are between twenty-five and fifty serial killers at work each year—"

"Twenty-five to fifty! Without being caught?" Diego said, those expressive eyes wide in disbelief.

"It was higher in the 1970s and '80s, when almost three hundred were active at one time. Many are eventually caught, like the alleged Long Island Serial Killer, who was recently arrested. But there are still open cases. The West Mesa Bone Collector investigation comes to mind," Gabriella said, and flipped the images on the screen to show maps marked to reflect the trails where the three women had been hiking.

Using a laser pointer, she circled it around the areas. "These locations are all less than ten miles apart. They're trails that would have been used by more experienced hikers."

"I don't want to be a wet blanket, but Selene Reilly disappeared not far from there. Not on a trail but still, it didn't turn out to be a serial killer," Robbie said, and closed the file that had been sitting in front of him.

Gabriella was familiar with the Reilly case. The local police and CBI had closed it as a suicide. If it hadn't been for her very determined twin sister and these SBS tech geniuses, Reilly might not have ever been freed from the mountain men who had abducted her. Still...

"Selene Reilly's case is an aberration. Sadly, in most disappearances, the victim is likely dead after forty-eight hours, but something inside me says Jeannie Roberts is still alive," she said, and skipped her gaze across all seated at the table, almost daring them to refuse the case.

The four gathered around the table all looked at one another, and then Sophie slowly came to her feet. "If you don't mind, Robbie and I would like a private word with Ryder."

"Of course. Shall Agent Rodriguez and I step outside?" she said, curbing her anger and worry.

Robbie popped to his feet and waved for them to stay. "We'll just go to my office," he said, and in a flurry of activity, the trio hurried out, leaving her staring at Diego.

"I get the feeling you're not on board with these all being related," she said, needing to know where he stood.

She didn't know why it mattered so much to her, but it did.

He shrugged impossibly broad shoulders and met her gaze. "Serial killers are above my pay grade, but I can tell you've done your research."

With a dip of her head to confirm it, she said, "I have. It's important to me that we not only solve these cases but find this missing hiker."

Diego narrowed his gaze and inspected her features, clearly assessing her. "I can tell it's important to you, but not just because of this missing hiker. Do you mind sharing why?"

The why of it wasn't something she normally shared with others, because it still hurt too much.

Luckily, she was spared from answering as the door opened and Robbie, Sophie and Ryder returned and sat at the table.

Sophie spoke up first. "We may not all agree with your serial killer theory, but we're all determined to find this missing hiker. If you're okay with that, Crooked Pass is eager to help."

It was less than she had hoped for, but she would take it. "I'm okay with that. Where do you want to start?"

JEANNIE HUGGED THE blanket tight, trying to stay warm against the cold from the stone walls and floor. The fact that he'd given her a blanket gave her hope that he intended to keep her alive for just a little longer.

She knew he didn't plan for her to leave this room alive. A large black bag sat in a far corner of the room. Large enough for a body.

Peering around in the dim light cast by the small overhead bulb, she searched for any way to escape besides the stairs off to one side of the room, but there were no windows or other openings.

Probably an old root cellar, she thought. That would explain the slight mustiness, dampness and constant chill.

Chill kept things from decaying.

Like a body, she thought, and fought back a sob.

She had to stay strong. She had to fight to survive. Whether it was for only another minute or another hour, the longer she stayed alive, the greater the likelihood the police would find her.

The creak of a door and slip of light from the top of the stairs warned he'd be joining her soon.

She sucked in a breath and prepared herself, bracing for his abuse. Praying that she had a clue on what pleased him so that he might keep her alive a little longer.

The bright lights, almost like stage lights, snapped on, jolting her into fearfulness.

The freak liked seeing her fear. But he also liked her fight as well.

As he came into view, face hidden beneath the black hood once again, she steadied herself and prayed.

Just let me live for one more minute, she thought. The minutes would become hours, and the hours might become another day of life.

It had to be enough for now, because help had to be on the way.

It just had to be.

Chapter Four

Since Crooked Pass Security had decided to help, Gabriella shared detailed information on all the individuals who had been interviewed in the prior cases. She placed their photos and basic data on the murder board at the front of the large conference room they were using as their war room.

As they reviewed the individuals and the bios of the missing women, they found connections between all three men and women to the local university.

"We'll reach out to the university's human resources department to see if they're willing to provide info on anyone employed during the time frames the women were there," Gabriella said, hoping that they would release the information without a warrant.

"What about getting info on any students in the classes that the women took?" Diego asked as he perused the photos on the board.

"Student privacy is regulated by FERPA," Ryder advised, and then tacked on, "The Family Educational Rights and Privacy Act."

"Which means we'll need a warrant," Diego said, and everyone around the table nodded.

"Right now, we don't have enough info to get a warrant," Gabriella said with a heavy sigh.

"But we have John Wilson's program, which is like a gigantic internet vacuum. He might be able to suck up enough info from publicly posted info to give us some leads," Sophie advised, and jotted down some notes on a pad.

"Do you think he could search their places of employment as well?" Gabriella asked.

Robbie nodded eagerly. "If it's out there, the program can bring it in."

"What about the hiking club that Roberts joined last year?" Diego asked as he flipped through the papers in the file the CBI agents had provided.

"Like I said, if the info is out there—" Robbie began, but Diego finished for him.

"The program can bring it in," he said, and waved his hand in apology. "Sorry, but I'm an old-school investigator."

Sophie smiled and said, "There's nothing wrong with boots on the ground. I think it's important to do that as well as using whatever technology is available."

"I agree," Gabriella said, and gazed in Diego's direction. "I'd like to revisit some of the earlier witness statements together and after, talk to these possible witnesses in person as well as the main persons of interest at the time."

"I'm game. If it's okay with you, I'd like to check out photos and maps of the trails at some point also," Diego said.

"It's okay with me," she said, and glanced around the table. "I understand that Wilson's program can also do a predictive analysis of possible suspects. Would it take long to run it against the current persons of interest and see what the program says?"

"We'll reach out to him and see if he can't prioritize that given the circumstances," Sophie said with a quick look at Robbie, who nodded to confirm that action.

"Great," Ryder said, stood and walked up to the murder board. Tapping the photos of the possible suspects and witnesses in the earlier cases, he said, "Let's split up these interviews."

Gabriella glanced at the board and considered the various individuals until one caught her eye. She walked up and pointed to his photo. "This was Cornerstone's boyfriend at the time of her disappearance. He would also have been at the university at the same time as all the missing women."

"The university has how many students at one time?" Diego tossed out for consideration.

"About five thousand. If there is a connection, it's likely because they had the same major or some other common interest like hiking," Gabriella responded, aware that the university connection might not amount to a pivotal clue.

Diego nodded. "Hiking for sure. I guess that's why I'd like to review those trails. See if they're dogworthy."

"Dogworthy?" Gabriella replied, a dark brow arched in question.

"Sorry for the lingo. It means checking out a crime scene to determine whether or not it's worth having my K-9 Poppy search," Diego explained.

"Got it. But the police search teams have already used their K-9s in the area where the hiker disappeared," Gabriella advised.

"I understand, but Poppy has exceptional skills. I'm also wondering about something," Diego said. He stood and approached the map.

Circling the area bounded by the locations of the three missing hikers, he said, "I don't know much about serial killers, but I know they sometimes keep all their victims in the same general area. They sometimes visit them also, right?"

Gabriella nodded and met Diego's dark gaze. "They do, but I believe that the serial killer is taking them to another location to kill them. If he does that, he may place them in an area far removed from where he took them."

An exasperated sigh escaped the K-9 agent, and he jammed his hands on his hips and examined the map again. After long seconds, he ran his finger along a main highway that circled the base of each of the trails. Glancing at Sophie and Robbie, he said, "Is there any possibility that CCTV cameras may have picked up any vehicles near these trailheads?"

"Possibly for the latest victim," Robbie replied.

"We're trying to get feeds from any traffic cameras in those areas," Ryder advised, and Gabriella confirmed.

"We should have them by later today."

"Great. Would you mind reviewing the trail photos and maps with me so we can decide whether to visit any of the locations before we get the bad weather that's coming in a few days?" Diego asked, and met her gaze, his intelligent and understanding.

"Sure, and after, we can meet with the possible persons of interest once Ryder and I decide who to take," she said.

"Great. I guess we should get going," he said with a glance at a large, military-style watch on his wrist.

"I have detailed maps and photos back in my office," she said, and then skipped her glance to those left at the table. "I guess we'll connect here later."

"Call us with an ETA and we'll bring in some dinner," Robbie said.

Sophie playfully elbowed him. "Ignore him. His belly is a bottomless pit that always needs filling."

"I'll be sure to keep that in mind," Gabriella said with a smile before returning her attention to Diego.

He did a small hand command and the large German shepherd, who had been peacefully lying by Diego's chair, head pillowed on big paws, rose and went to Diego's side.

Motioning to the door of the conference room with his hand, he said, "Lead the way."

IT WAS A short drive from the new offices of Crooked Pass Security in downtown Denver to the CBI offices in nearby Lakewood. After clearing security, Diego followed Gabriella to the elevators and then to her spacious office.

The office immediately said a lot about her.

Everything was neat and orderly, including the murder board at one end of the room that was virtually a replica of the one they'd set up back at the Crooked Pass Security offices.

Her desktop had a black blotter edged with a very feminine floral pattern. A few desk accessories matched the blotter. Beside them, a picture frame held a photo that he couldn't see from his position in front of the desk. An expensive-looking silver-and-gold pen set sat at the top of the blotter. A file with papers occupied the middle of the blotter.

Gabriella went to her chair, removed her suit jacket and draped it over the back of her chair.

The action drew attention to the shoulder holster and Glock tucked within as well as the way the fine cotton of her blouse cradled generous breasts.

That dichotomy of femininity and power was a heady aphrodisiac, and he had to drag his attention away from her. His focus had to be on the case and proving himself, and not the very attractive CBI agent with the shadows of sadness in her eyes.

He rubbed Poppy's head in reward and gestured for her to sit, which she did with a bored sigh. His K-9 was used to more activity, and he'd have to take her for a long walk later to let her stretch her legs.

Gabriella swung around her desk, picked up the file crammed with a large stack of papers and tucked it against her chest.

She laid the file on top of a small nearby table and with a wave of a hand, invited him to sit.

He did, and she joined him, sitting beside him so they could both look at the materials as she spread them out and identified each of them.

"You asked to see photos of the trails. These are from the most recent disappearance," she said, and pointed out a big boulder. "We suspect Roberts was nearly at the summit when she stopped to appreciate the view and have a snack."

"And he grabbed her there? Is that what you think?" Diego asked, wanting to understand what CBI thought about the hiker's movements.

Gabriella ran a long, elegant finger with a bright red nail along the image of the boulder in the photo. "There were scattered remnants of trail mix here. That would support that hypothesis."

"And he—I assume it's a he—" he said, and met her gaze, awaiting her confirmation.

"Most serial killers are male, white, and between the ages of twenty-five and thirty-four," she advised.

That represented a large swath of the population of Denver, he thought. Motioning to the photos of the trail, he said, "He grabs her and forcefully takes her back down the mountain. No one sees them."

"No one, although we had a couple of callers say that they saw Roberts's car in the parking lot for the trailhead but didn't see her. There weren't that many people on the trail, possibly due to the unseasonable snow we recently had," she explained.

"This trail goes higher than others in the area, so there might still be snow there. I saw it myself when I hiked it," he said, and tacked on, "How did he know she was doing the hike?"

Gabriella's full lips tightened into a thin line, and she did a little shrug. "Serial killers generally go through phases. One of them is trolling, where they seek out a victim. Usually, they do it in an area where they are likely to meet the kind of person that attracts them, like the university."

"Why wouldn't he grab her there?" he wondered aloud, and shifted away the photos from the Roberts trail to those from one of the earlier disappearances.

He noticed right away that the trails looked very similar, so maybe hiking them was where the serial killer might meet his victim. If it even was a serial killer, he thought, recalling Ryder's reticence about that theory.

"The university might be too public a place for a grab. He might woo them there, though. That's another phase. The serial killer tries to ingratiate himself to his victim to create a level of comfort or confidence with them," Gabriella explained, and handed him the photos from the very first disappearance.

"There wasn't much evidence from the first two trails, either because they didn't see them as a crime scene or because the killer was careful," she explained, and sat back in her chair with a heavy sigh.

He understood her dejection. If she was right, two women had already lost their lives, and the third...

"I wish I could say these other trails are dogworthy, but it's been nearly two years since the women were on these trails," he said, and gathered up the photos of those areas, but as he did so, he noticed another set of pictures in her file.

He reached for them, but she stayed his hand with hers. He noticed her hand tremble as she did so and heard her say in a soft tone, "That one's not pertinent right now."

He wondered at her reticence about that location but honored her request. For the moment, at least.

"Ryder isn't on board with your theory because of the gap between these disappearances. Why do you think they're connected?" he pressed, wanting to know her mind and how it worked.

"As I mentioned earlier, there have been gaps before. It happens because the killer almost always takes a trophy from the victim and uses that to relive the experience. But as the adrenaline wears off, that phase fades. The killer then becomes depressed. That depression can last for a long time until he starts to fantasize again and then starts trolling once more," she explained.

"And that trophy and depression phase could account for the two-year gap?" he asked.

She nodded. "It could explain it according to all my research."

"Would you mind sharing any of the research so I can get up to speed on your theory?" he asked, wanting to be as helpful as possible during their investigation.

"I don't mind. I'll have my assistant make copies of my notes so you can review them," she said, and gathered up the photos into her file.

Before he could say anything else, she shot to her feet, marched to her murder board and rapped her knuckles against its surface. "The clock is ticking, and I worry that once he murders her, we'll lose his trail until he takes another victim. That's why we need to interview these people as soon as possible."

Her gaze gleamed with determination but also that sadness he had seen earlier that day. He understood the determination. As for the sadness, he hoped he'd one day understand what had put it there.

Pushing to his feet, he said, "Whatever you need to do, I'm ready to help."

Chapter Five

Gabriella shot a quick look at Diego as he sat beside her in the SUV. His K-9 Poppy was harnessed in the back seat, peacefully sitting there.

They'd let Poppy scent a dirty T-shirt that Roberts's mother had provided from the missing woman's apartment after the police had released the area as a crime scene. Diego now had the plastic bag that held the T-shirt so that Poppy could take another sniff before they met up with each of the three suspects they were visiting. In the meantime, Gabriella's partner Ryder would speak to the witnesses from each of the disappearances.

She'd seen what scent dogs could do on other cases with the CBI but wondered if Poppy could help them on this case.

"Do you think she can pick up Roberts's scent if one of these men is responsible for her disappearance?" Gabriella asked, and watched Diego's reaction from the corner of her eye.

He did a little side-to-side bobble of his head, as if uncertain, and then said, "Possibly. Poppy has a strong sense of smell and if one of them has been near Roberts recently, she might pick it up."

If she did, they could focus on that suspect and maybe even find Roberts before she was murdered.

Gabriella was sure that Roberts was still alive.

But not for long.

While the killer was likely enjoying his time with her, he also had to know that he couldn't keep her for much longer.

Gabriella was convinced that was his MO. Abduct, hold, murder and then dump them far removed from the original location. That explained why the bodies of the first two women had yet to be found.

But what about Isabella? the little voice in her head challenged. If Isabella was the first, was his MO the same or different? Was it possible her sister lay somewhere not far from the missing women?

"How long does a cadaver's scent linger?" she asked aloud, wondering if Poppy could pick up the smell of a body that was nearly eight years old.

With a shrug of his broad shoulders, Diego said, "Dogs have been known to pick up scents that have been in the ground for decades. Sometimes even millennia."

"Millennia?" Gabriella pressed, dubious of the claim.

Diego nodded without hesitation. "Archaeologists have used dogs to find remains at various dig sites."

So it wasn't so far-fetched that they might be able to find her little sister after nearly a decade. But only if they could make some headway on this case.

"Our victims are more recent, so hopefully we can identify a possible killing field," she said, and checked her rearview mirror before pulling into the parking lot for the office building for Cornerstone's former boyfriend, Maxwell Baxter.

"Cornerstone disappeared about six months after graduation. Baxter and she had been dating for over a year. They were both business majors, which was how they'd met," Gabriella advised as she parked in front of the nondescript glass-and-cement building in the small corporate center.

Diego turned slightly in his seat to face her and said, "I only got a quick look at the file, but it seemed to me that the police and CBI ruled him out as a person of interest fairly quickly."

Gabriella met his gaze and nodded. "They did. He had an alibi, but I'm not convinced," she said, and wrinkled her nose.

"I guess you don't think it passes the smell test," he gathered from her gesture.

"His alibi is another woman. He was cheating on Cornerstone with her and as far as I'm concerned, that's as good as lying," she said with a determined bob of her head.

Diego didn't disagree. "Once a liar, always a liar."

"Definitely. Not to mention that I didn't interview him, and I'd like to get my own take on him."

"And Poppy's take if she can pick up Roberts's scent," Diego added.

"That's right. If you're ready, let's go interview Cornerstone's cheating boyfriend," Gabriella said, and slipped out of the car.

Diego stepped out and then opened the back door to release Poppy. The German shepherd hopped out, and Diego grabbed her leash. Together they followed Gabriella along the path to the front door of the office of a well-known accounting firm.

As they entered the lobby, the receptionist, a young, pretty twentysomething, greeted them with a warm smile. "How may we help you today?"

Gabriella pulled her CBI badge from a leather cross-body bag, held it up for the receptionist to see and said, "We'd like to speak with Maxwell Baxter."

The warm smile faded instantly. "I'll see if he's available."

Diego knew that Baxter would be available whether or not he wanted to be, but didn't say it, certain Gabriella could handle the situation if Baxter refused to cooperate.

The receptionist dialed Baxter and in a whisper into her headset, explained the situation. Barely a second later, she ended the call and said, "Through those double doors. Mr. Baxter's office is the third one to the right."

"Thank you," Gabriella said, and he trailed behind her, Poppy leashed tight to his leg.

They walked in together to find Baxter standing just outside the door to his office.

He hadn't aged much in the nearly three years since Cornerstone's disappearance, Diego thought, recalling the photo from Gabriella's file.

His blond hair was cut in a similar fade, but the T-shirt and jeans were gone, replaced by a bespoke suit befitting someone in an upscale accounting firm. He had a preppy, pretty-boy look that immediately set Diego's teeth on edge. He'd had too many of those types look down their noses at someone like him, a working-class kid who'd paid his way through college as a marine ROTC.

"Please come in," Baxter said, and held his hand out in invitation, a forced smile on his features.

As soon as they had stepped in, he closed the door behind them and hurried to his desk. He sat down and, in a tone as icy as his light blue gaze, he said, "What can I do for you?"

"We're investigating Missy Cornerstone's disappearance," Gabriella said.

Baxter's gaze narrowed and drifted from Gabriella to him and then to Poppy.

"I thought Missy's case was closed," he said.

"The case will only be closed once we find Missy and know what happened to her," Gabriella said.

"I had nothing to do with that," Baxter immediately countered.

"Great. Then you won't mind answering a few questions for me," Gabriella said and began rattling off a standard series of questions about his relationship with Missy and the events on the day she disappeared.

As she did so, Diego watched Baxter closely, trying to pick up any signs of deception. But he failed to notice anything.

Baxter's gaze stayed glued to Gabriella for the most part, except for a look in Diego's direction when she mentioned his cheating. It was almost as if Baxter was hoping for some kind of kinship since Diego was another man and might condone his actions.

When he didn't get the intended response, Baxter focused on Gabriella again, answering without hesitation or any of the little tells Diego had learned over the years as an investigator and K-9 handler.

After about a half hour of Gabriella's questioning, Baxter grew frustrated. Especially as she grilled him for yet another time with a similar question to one he had already answered, hoping to elicit a different, and possibly deceptive, response.

Baxter sat up straighter and splayed his hands on his desktop. "Agent Ruiz, I've already answered that question, and if you don't mind, I have to end this. I have a client coming in shortly and need to prepare for that meeting."

Gabriella hesitated but then rose, reached into her bag and handed him her business card. "I appreciate you taking the time to chat with us. If you can think of anything else, please call."

Baxter slipped it into his desk drawer. "I will. Believe me, I want to find Missy as much as you do. I want that sword to stop hanging over my head," he said, rose and walked to the door of his office.

When he opened it, Gabriella walked there and glanced in his direction, her meaning clear.

He stood and urged Poppy to heel with a slight tug at her leash, but at the door, he gave Poppy a hand signal to scent Baxter.

She did, sniffing all around him for long seconds until Baxter stepped away and swiped at his pants leg as if Poppy had left something nasty behind. Baxter was clearly not a fan of dogs.

"I need to get to work," Baxter reiterated, and Diego repeated Gabriella's earlier thanks.

"We appreciate you answering our questions," he said as

Gabriella and he walked out the door, Poppy just slightly behind them.

Gabriella leaned close as they walked. In heels, she was about a head shorter than him, and her silky hair brushed the underside of his jaw as she whispered, "Did Poppy pick up on anything?"

"Nothing," he said, and battled the physical response to her proximity and the smell of her, a flowery and citrusy perfume mixed with the slight odor of leather from her holster.

He willed away the attraction, and if she noticed, he didn't pick up on it as they walked to her car and he secured Poppy in the back seat once again.

"What was your read of Baxter?" she asked as she slipped behind the wheel and started the car.

"Besides his being a cheating prick who still doesn't get why that was wrong?" he said, recalling how the man had looked at him during the interview.

"Besides that," Gabriella said with a half smile and chuckle as she pulled out of the parking spot.

"He wasn't lying, and I do think he'd love for us to figure out what happened to Missy. Not for her or her family, but because it lets him off the hook. That's all that matters to people like him," he said with some bite in his tone.

She immediately picked up on it and peeked in his direction. "You've had your run-ins with the Baxters of the world?"

"You might say that, but you probably have as well," he said, deflecting because he wasn't ready to share more about himself. At least not until he knew more about her.

"I have. People who are born on third base sometimes tend to think the world should revolve around them," she said, dragging a chuckle from him.

"Third base people. I like that and yes, Baxter is definitely self-centered, but does that make him a killer?"

Gabriella gripped the steering wheel tightly and shrugged,

her lips in a tight slash. "Serial killers can be egotistical. Just look at Bundy thinking he could represent himself at his murder trial."

Even he knew that about Bundy, although he still had to read through the notes she had provided.

"I guess Baxter stays on the list of suspects for now," he said, just to be sure they were on the same page.

"He does. Next up is Nations's old boyfriend, and then we're off to see Roberts's current partner."

"Did you notice that Baxter didn't seem to like Poppy too much?" he asked.

"I did. Why?" she asked with a glance in his direction.

With a laugh he replied, "I think Bill Murray said that he was suspicious of people who didn't like dogs, but trusted when a dog didn't like a person."

Laughter exploded from Gabriella, and she looked at Poppy. "I like that. I can't wait to see what Poppy thinks of the next two suspects."

"I can't either," he said, and settled in for the short drive to their next destination.

Chapter Six

The interview with Ben Kinston went much like the one with Maxwell Baxter.

Kinston clearly hadn't been happy to see them on the doorstep of his small veterinary practice, especially since he seemed to be having a very busy day with an assortment of sick and injured pets.

Despite that, he took the time to chat about his former girlfriend Alyssa Nations. When he was shown pictures of Cornerstone, Nations and Roberts, he indicated he had no knowledge of them and had never seen them in his classes.

That made sense to Diego, since all three of the women had been business majors while Kinston had taken biology. As they were leaving, it was obvious Poppy hadn't picked up Roberts's scent on Kinston and that she liked the vet, especially when he asked permission to rub her head and give her a treat.

Diego appreciated that he understood that working dogs weren't pets.

Since the vet had a nice dog park adjacent to his office building, Diego said, "Do you mind if I let Poppy relieve herself and have some downtime?"

"Not at all. It would be nice to stretch my legs and get some fresh air," she said as they exited the vet's office.

He nodded and walked with Poppy to the dog park. The area was empty as most of the dogs were inside, awaiting treatment.

He removed the leash from Poppy's harness and with a hand command, set her free to relieve herself.

The German shepherd took off, racing to the far end of the dog park to do her duty. When she was done, she raced around the park, speeding up and down some of the ramps playfully.

"It's good to see her acting like a regular dog," Gabriella said as he grabbed a waste bag from a nearby holder, and strolled with him to pick up Poppy's mess.

"It is. I feel for her when we're caught up in some investigation and she's trapped in a room."

GABRIELLA PEERED IN his direction, sensing that he also didn't like being trapped for hours. Which made her wonder aloud, "How did you become a K-9 handler?"

With a shrug, he said, "It just happened."

He also wasn't someone who liked to share about himself, but Gabriella was determined to know more because he intrigued her.

"How did you end up working with Crooked Pass Security?" she asked as they reached the back of the dog park, and he bent to pick up Poppy's waste.

He didn't face her as he said, "I knew Sophie and Robbie from some other cases we worked together. A friend knew they were hiring and suggested I meet with them."

"You worked with Ryder as well, didn't you?" she asked as he straightened and closed the waste bag.

"I did. How long have you known Ryder?" he asked, and since he'd opened up a little about himself, she did the same.

"For about six years. I interned with CBI while I was in college and once I graduated, I was offered a position with them."

"He seems like a good guy and from what I can see, Sophie and he are a good match," Diego said.

"They are. It's not easy to find that when you work in law enforcement. The demands of the job put a strain on relationships."

"Is that why you're single?" he said, and glanced at her from the corner of his eye as they walked back toward the dog park entrance.

"Who said I'm single?" she teased. She loved the flash of disappointment across his face before she put him out of his misery.

"I'm single. Not looking at the moment but if it were to happen—"

She didn't get to finish as he let out an earsplitting whistle and Poppy came running over.

The whistle was payback, she surmised from the boyish grin on his face as he rubbed Poppy's head and body before slipping her a treat.

As he leashed Poppy, he schooled his features as he said, "On to our last suspect?"

"On to Peter Konijn. Poppy is likely going to scent Roberts on him since they're currently involved," she said as they walked back to the car to visit the last suspect.

"Does he have an alibi for the day Roberts went missing?" Diego asked, brow furrowed as he waited for her answer.

"He claims he was visiting his parents, and they confirm it," she advised, and unlocked the car doors.

Once they were seated, he said, "But you don't believe that."

"Parents protect their children. That might include lying for them," she answered without hesitation.

"Even if they know he's lying and could be a killer?" Diego challenged.

Gabriella tapped her forehead in emphasis. "They might suspect it up here, but don't want to believe it. Maybe with the right proof they would come clean."

Diego was silent for a long moment before he said, "If their son did take Roberts, their lies could be endangering her life."

She couldn't argue with that. "I know Ryder is interviewing the parents, but I may want to talk to them myself depending on the read I get from Konijn today."

"I don't blame you. Especially since the clock is ticking," he said, and captured her gaze for a hot second before she had to return her attention to the road.

The clock was ticking, so she wasted no time in getting to the Konijn family offices, which were luckily not far from Sixteenth Street and the CPS location.

"Another third-baser," Diego said as he took in the fancy brass plaque at the door that said Konijn Wealth Management.

A wry smile drifted across Gabriella's lips, and it hit him that she was even more beautiful when she smiled, lighting up her dark brown eyes. As she thanked him for opening the door and their gazes connected, he felt gobsmacked again and as her eyes widened slightly, she was obviously feeling that connection as well.

The lobby for the Konijn family business screamed money, from the gleaming mahogany wood of the receptionist's desk to the artwork on the walls. He wasn't an expert, but it didn't take one to identify a signed Warhol print on one wall and what looked like a Jackson Pollock behind the receptionist's desk.

As she had before, Gabriella approached the desk and was met with the same resistance as at Baxter's location. But the badge made things happen again and within seconds, a young man emerged from the office area.

"Mr. Konijn asked that I show you to our conference room," he said, and motioned to a door just to the left and behind the receptionist's area. Clearly, Konijn didn't want anyone to see them.

They followed him into the conference room where with an obsequious smile and clutch of his hands, the man said, "Is there anything I can get you? Water? Coffee, perhaps?"

"Just Mr. Konijn," Gabriella said, her tone making it clear she wasn't pleased with the wait.

The man's smile faded. He nodded and replied, "He'll be right with you."

He hurried from the room and barely a minute later, Peter Konijn walked in by an older man who had to be his father. They had a similar build and facial features. The older Konijn's hair had gone mostly white, but here and there were remnants of his son's sandy-colored hair.

Peter walked over, a grim look on his face. "Peter Konijn. My father, Ralph Konijn," he said as he first shook Gabriella's hand and then his.

It's not parent-teacher night, Gabriella thought as father and son sat at the conference room table. The elder Konijn took the head of the table with his son to the right.

"There's no need for your father to be present," she said, and sat across from Peter, wanting to see every reaction to her questions.

"Actually, there is. I'm also an attorney and here to make sure my son's rights are protected," the older man said with an imperial arch of a silvery brow.

"Then you'll appreciate that your son is not in custody and as such, anything he says right now can and will be used against him. If he chooses not to answer my questions, I'll take him in for a formal interview. Would you prefer that?" she said, not about to be steamrolled by Peter's father.

The older man sputtered and was about to reply when Peter laid a warning hand on his jacket sleeve.

"I've got nothing to hide, Father. Ask away, Agent Ruiz," he said, and offered her an apologetic smile.

"Great," she said, and ran through his statement about his whereabouts on the day his partner disappeared.

His response didn't deviate from the earlier facts that she'd received, even when she pressed him a second and third time about what he'd done that day.

"My son has already answered repeatedly, and my wife and I can confirm his whereabouts," Ralph Konijn chimed in, words clipped with anger.

Gabriella silenced him with a glare, and a red flush of rage swept across his features.

Satisfied with Peter's answers, she shot a quick look at Diego, who whipped out the photos of the two other missing women. He placed them in front of Peter.

Peter narrowed his eyes and examined the photos.

"I don't understand," he said, and met her gaze, puzzlement on his.

"Do you recognize either of these women?" she asked.

He dipped his head from side to side, considering her question, and after a slight hesitation, he tapped one photo. "She looks familiar. Maybe from DU?" he said, the doubt obvious from his tone.

"Her name is Alyssa Nations. She disappeared two years ago from a trail not far from where Jeannie disappeared. The other woman is Missy Cornerstone. She likewise disappeared from a hiking trail," she advised.

The blood fled from both father's and son's faces. A second later, Peter waved his hands in denial. "I know nothing about these two women."

"They were both business majors at DU. Alyssa was the same year as you and Jeannie. Missy was two years behind you, but maybe you took similar classes," Gabriella advised, and after another nod at Diego, he placed more photos of the women in front of Peter.

Peter didn't look at them. He just waved his hands again and said, "There are hundreds if not thousands of business majors. We may have crossed paths at DU, but that's about it. I don't know anything about them."

She was tempted to press him about the disappearance dates for the two women but decided to switch back to Roberts.

"Do you and Jeannie have a good relationship?" she asked as she swept up the photos of the other missing women.

"We do. We've been dating since junior year and moved

in together about six months ago," Peter advised, and relaxed slightly.

"Moving in together is a big life change. How's that going?" she asked, making her tone almost friendly to lull him into a false sense of security.

"Well. We have many shared interests and friends. Jeannie was very detail oriented, and so am I," he said.

She didn't fail to miss the "was" instead of "is."

"I gather hiking wasn't one of those 'shared interests'?" she pressed.

"It is, only... I had promised my parents I'd visit that weekend," he said, and shot a nervous look at his father as if needing reassurance.

"A visit without Jeannie?" she questioned, wondering why Roberts wouldn't have gone with him.

Peter swallowed awkwardly and nervously glanced at his father yet again.

Ralph answered for his son, his tone glacial. "My wife and I didn't always see eye to eye with Ms. Roberts."

Now this was getting interesting, Diego thought as he glanced from the Konijns to Gabriella.

"What about?" she pressed.

"It's a family matter I'd rather not discuss in front of strangers," Ralph advised, his face as stony as granite.

"Would you rather discuss it at CBI offices?" she threatened again.

After a strangled cough, Peter said, "Jeannie thought I should spread my wings and work with another firm before settling for working with the family."

"Settling is not what I would call working for a top wealth management firm," his father immediately challenged.

"I know, Father. But maybe—"

"There's no maybes here, and this is not something to discuss in front of strangers," his father said to shut down the discussion.

Interesting, he thought. Dad likely had more reason for Roberts to disappear than the son.

A pained silence followed until Gabriella said, "I think that's all we need for now."

She rose and as she did so, she met his gaze and dipped her head in the direction of both father and son.

When the Konijns stood, Diego shot to his feet and motioned to Poppy, who eagerly responded, ready to act.

Gabriella waited as he slipped behind her and positioned himself and Poppy at the door. He gestured for the Konijns to exit, and they hesitated, but he insisted. "Please, you go first."

Ralph Konijn moved toward them and as he neared, Diego instructed Poppy to scent him.

The dog sniffed the father's legs, and he shied away, as if afraid of the dog.

"I'm sorry, I don't care for dogs," he said, and hurried past. Poppy lay down, signaling that she'd scented Roberts.

A second later, Peter walked by and Poppy rose, sniffed him and lay down again. Not surprising considering that Peter and Jeannie lived together.

But Poppy's reaction to Ralph was a different thing, and Gabriella had picked up on it.

As they walked into the lobby, she asked the elder Konijn, "When was the last time you saw Ms. Roberts?"

The older man glanced at his son, clearly discomfited, and said, "I can't say. Several weeks ago, I think."

"Weeks? Are you sure about that?" Diego said, certain from Poppy's reaction that it had to be more recent.

The two men shared a look, and this time Peter answered. "Weeks. As you might have guessed, Jeannie didn't visit with my parents often."

"If you could recall when that might be, I'd appreciate knowing the date," Gabriella said, and handed Peter her business card.

Peter fingered the card and then nodded. "I'll check my calendar and let you know."

"Great. Thanks," she said, whirled on a high-heeled foot and strode toward the door, Diego following her.

There was a pep in her step that said she was pleased with the outcome of the interview.

As they settled in the car, Poppy harnessed in the back seat, she met his gaze and said, "What did you think?"

"I think you have another suspect to add to your list."

She smiled and nodded. "I agree."

Chapter Seven

He'd been surprised at the arrival of the CBI agent and her K-9 sidekick.

He didn't like surprises.

He tapped the business card on his tabletop, wondering how she had connected the disappearances of the three women.

Granted, a good cop should have made the connections between Cornerstone and Nations sooner. But they hadn't.

Most cops were idiots, which was why he'd felt safe grabbing Roberts.

But somehow this CBI agent had put two and two together.

He peered at the business card again.

Gabriella Ruiz. The Ruiz name popped out at him like a big flashing warning sign.

He hadn't known her name when he'd first taken her.

But in the days after her disappearance, her name had been plastered all over the news.

Isabella Ruiz.

Ruiz, just like the beautiful CBI agent who had visited today.

He closed his eyes and pictured the twelve-year-old who'd awakened him to his true calling.

She'd had dark hair and eyes as well, but then again, many Latinas had similar coloring.

He screwed his eyes closed tighter, trying to remember more, but the memories had grown slightly fuzzy over the years. He couldn't remember if her nose had been as pert and straight as that of the CBI agent. Or if she'd had that smallish dimple in her chin.

He should have taken a photo of her, but her kill had been too new and exciting, and he'd been too inexperienced.

He'd been better prepared for the others. Their photos were carefully tucked away with the small mementos he'd taken from them.

But he had a few mementos from Isabella. A small gold crucifix. A lock of her dark hair. The childish bracelet, like something out of a Cracker Jack box, that said, "Best friends."

There was no way the CBI agent was related to Isabella. No way. Ruiz had to be a common name.

But just in case, he intended to find out more about the attractive CBI agent.

And if she was related to Isabella...

That would only make things even more interesting.

GABRIELLA PARKED THE car a few doors down from the building for the Crooked Pass Security offices, but Diego wasn't ready to head upstairs to meet just yet.

"I'll meet you at the offices in about fifteen minutes. I need to walk Poppy," he said as he freed the German shepherd from the back seat.

"I could use a little fresh air as well," Gabriella said, and arched her back in a stretch that had him looking at all the wrong places.

He dragged his gaze away and muttered, "Suit yourself."

She gave him a side-eyed glance, puzzled by his almost snarky tone, and he apologized. After all, it wasn't her fault he was finding her way too attractive.

"I'm sorry. I mean, don't feel obligated to stay with us. I know you probably have a lot of work to do."

"I do, but if we're going to work together, I thought it would be good to get to know each other," she said, and joined him on the sidewalk.

"Sure," he said as he leashed Poppy and leisurely walked to the end of the block and onto the pedestrian Sixteenth Street Mall.

Gabriella matched his pace as she said, "You said you just kinda became a K-9 handler. Was it in the...did I hear you used to be a marine?"

"I *am* a marine. Once a marine, always a marine," he said with a smile and shake of his head.

A ghost of a smile drifted across her face, but it was tinged with that hint of sadness again. "I should have remembered that. My dad was...is...a marine."

"You said 'was.' Did he pass?" Diego wondered, deciding to use the walk to learn more about her as well.

She shook her head. "No, he's still alive. It's just that...things are a little weird between us," she admitted.

He didn't press, certain that the weirdness might be the source of her sadness. Before he could ask her another question, she said, "Why the Marines?"

"My grandfather was a marine in Vietnam, and I wanted to follow in his footsteps and help protect my country. It also helped pay for college."

She glanced at him from the corner of her eye. "It's not easy to get one of those ROTC scholarships."

Bragging wasn't his thing so with a shrug, he said, "It just kinda—"

"Happened," she finished for him and then tacked on, "Why not stay in the Marines? Didn't you finish ROTC as an officer?"

He nodded. "Second lieutenant. I shipped overseas to Afghanistan. Did my two years there."

"Just the two? No marine career for you?" she pressed just as Poppy relieved herself, letting him break from a discussion that might be too revealing. The last thing he wanted to do was share how PTSD had derailed his military career and defined his civilian life for way too long.

He pulled a waste bag from his jacket pocket, cleaned it up and deposited it in a nearby garbage can.

When he faced her, her gaze had narrowed, and he realized she was still expecting a response from him.

"No career for me. We should head back to CPS. They're probably wondering where we are, and Robbie is probably gnawing the conference room table," he said, and gestured in the direction of the Crooked Pass Security building.

GABRIELLA DIDN'T MISS that Diego didn't want to talk about his stint as a marine. For the moment, she left that alone, much like he didn't push when she'd mentioned her rift with her father.

A rift caused by the turmoil that had followed her sister's disappearance.

"Sure," she said, and they walked back to the CPS offices. They reached the doors at the same time as a deliveryman from a local Mexican restaurant.

When the man entered the elevator with them and hit the button for the CPS offices, Diego said, "We can take that up for you."

"No thanks, mano. That Robbie is a great tipper," the man said, and rode up to the offices with them.

Diego badged them in and a second later, apparently hearing the thunk of the front door lock, Robbie poked his head out of the conference room.

"Jamie, mano," Robbie said.

Jamie, the delivery man, passed Robbie one of the bags and waited for Robbie to tip him before handing the second bag to Diego.

"See you soon," Jamie said and hit the door button to exit the offices.

"I guess Jamie's a regular?" Gabriella said with a chuckle.

"Robbie's half-Cuban but has a thing for Mexican food," Diego said as they followed Robbie into the conference room where Ryder and Sophie were clearing the surface of the table.

"I get it. I always love it when my mami makes Mexican food," she said with a smile, recalling the tamales, menudo and pozole her mother had cooked just a few months ago for their Christmas Eve meal.

"Hopefully you won't be disappointed," he said, and removed the take-out dishes from the bag.

"We didn't know what you would want, so we ordered a lot of different things," Sophie said as she walked over with plates, cutlery and napkins while Robbie laid out an assortment of drinks on a credenza off to one side of the room.

In no time they were serving themselves from the dishes filled with hearty rice and black beans, assorted tacos, and the tamales, which were always one of her favorites.

Diego had grabbed one as well and at her questioning glance, since many people didn't like the cornmeal consistency, he said, "They're a lot like our Cuban tamales."

Plate loaded with food, but not enough to make her sleepy since they had a night of work ahead, she sat at the table, and Diego placed his plate by hers. A second later, he returned with two sodas, and she thanked him.

Silence reigned around the table for only a few minutes before Sophie glanced between them and Ryder and said, "How did your interviews go?"

Gabriella motioned to Ryder, wanting to defer their discussion since the addition of Ralph Konijn to their suspect list would likely be a surprise.

"Witness statements haven't changed much except for one thing. Alyssa Nations's former roommate remembered that Alyssa had been a little spooked in the days just before her disappearance."

Gabriella paused with her fork halfway to her mouth and

straightened in her seat. "Did she know why Alyssa was spooked?"

"She said that Alyssa mentioned that she thought someone was following her," Ryder advised.

His comment was almost like a punch to her gut, because one of Isabella's scout mates had told her something similar years after her sister's disappearance. She laid the food-laden fork down with a shaky hand.

"Did her roommate see anyone around that was suspicious?" she asked.

Ryder shook his head. "She says that she wished she'd paid more attention when Alyssa said it, but she didn't recall anything out of the ordinary."

"Nothing similar from Missy's witnesses?" Diego asked, and forked up some tamale.

"No. I've hit everyone on the current list, and I'm hoping that the Miami SBS branch can help with Wilson's program," Ryder advised.

"We just got the SBS reports a few minutes ago. We can take a look when you're ready," Robbie said around a mouthful of food.

His plate was piled high, and it made Gabriella remember what Diego had said about Robbie being a bottomless pit.

Beside Robbie, Sophie and Ryder sat side by side, shoulders brushing occasionally, clearly now a couple. In the few weeks since they'd met, she'd seen a decided change in her colleague. He seemed happier and often left the office with a smile, eager to go home.

Which for some reason had her shooting a glance at Diego.

There was no doubt he was handsome. Troubled, she thought, recognizing a kindred spirit that way. Maybe that was the reason for the instant connection she'd felt.

"How did your interviews go?" Ryder asked, his gaze drifting between her and Diego.

Diego did a little shrug and deferred to her, peering in her direction.

"Kinston's clear in my book," she said, and Diego nodded in agreement.

"Baxter's not the nicest guy, but I'd drop him down on the list. That leaves Konijn," she said, and again got a nod from Diego.

"There's something in your tone that says you're not eliminating him just yet," Sophie said.

Diego and she shared a quick look before she said, "Actually, it looks like we may be adding a new suspect."

Chapter Eight

Jeannie tugged and pulled at the one metal shackle, trying to free herself. Her skin was almost raw from trying to slip her hand through the band, but she had to keep on trying.

She understood now why some animals would gnaw off a leg to escape a hunter's trap.

Try as she might, she couldn't work her hand past the metal cuff around her wrist.

What was the sense anyway? she asked herself with a frustrated sob. Even if she freed her hand, there were still three other restraints keeping her prisoner.

A cellar with only one way out that was right past her captor.

Footsteps sounded above her.

He was home.

Cold filled her gut, and she drew her arms and legs tight, fearing his arrival.

A second later, a sliver of light warned he was opening a trapdoor at the top of the stairs.

The light grew brighter as he lifted it ever higher and then stepped down into the cellar.

There was something different about his pace. It was slower. More deliberate.

Would this be her last day? she wondered.

As he reached the bottom of the stairs, he flipped on the lights, nearly blinding her after a day spent in the darkness of the cellar.

"Good evening, Jeannie," he said, surprising her. She hadn't thought that he knew her name.

At her continued silence, he slipped out the knife and said, "It's usually polite to say 'Good evening' back."

Since she'd learned he liked a little fight, she tilted her chin up a defiant inch and said, "Good evening, back."

He laughed, a loud, hearty laugh, and sheathed the knife.

"I see you're learning. That's a good little toy, Jeannie," he said, and whipped up the camera.

"Look at me," he said, and when she did, he snapped off a few photos.

She waited for his next command, waited for him to undress and take her, and when he didn't, she held her breath, wondering yet again if this would be her last day of life.

Instead, he sniffed the air and said, "I can smell your fear. It's intoxicating."

He walked over then, fully dressed, bent, and buried his face against the side of her neck.

As he did so, she realized the Bowie knife was within easy reach.

She shot out her hand to grab it, but he was faster and snared her hand before she could grab it and plunge it into his heart.

He twisted her wrist, making her cry out from the pain.

He only laughed and said, "See how easy it is to want to kill someone?"

With another rough twist, her wrist snapped, and pain exploded through her body.

She moaned, but he only laughed and stepped away.

Cradling her broken wrist to her chest, she watched as he backed away toward the stairs.

"I like your fight, Jeannie. But tonight, I have something more important to do," he said. He whirled, shut off the bright lights and hurried up the steps.

Tears of pain and joy spilled down her face.

She was broken, but she was still alive.

That was all that mattered.

ROBBIE AND SOPHIE had sent Ralph Konijn's name to their Miami counterparts to get whatever information they could about the older man.

In the meantime, Diego, Ryder and Gabriella cleared off the table of their dinner remnants and tackled the information that John Wilson had sent.

Diego glanced at the reports, trying to absorb the wealth of details gathered about not only their three possible suspects but several other individuals that the three victims might have in common.

It was almost too much information, and Diego worried that it might delay them rather than help.

"This is a lot to take in," he said as he flipped through all the reports.

"It is, but let's go through each suspect and see if the analysis agrees with our initial observations," Sophie said as she turned on a monitor on one wall of the room and brought up Wilson's report.

As she did so, Gabriella rose and walked to their murder board to transfer any pertinent information there.

"Wilson's predictive program has assigned a low probability score to both Baxter and Kinston. Do you both agree with that?" Sophie said, and skipped her glance from him to Gabriella.

At Gabriella's nod, he said, "We agree."

"Konijn was slightly higher at 65 percent but in my mind, that's still a failing grade," Ryder said as he, too, skimmed through the papers.

"And how does Wilson even get to these numbers?" Diego wondered aloud.

"Sophie can show you," Robbie said. With that, his sister

scrolled through a few screens to bring up one that had a breakdown of various factors that Wilson's program had considered.

"As we mentioned earlier, John's program is like a giant internet vacuum, sucking up whatever information it can from various sources and analyzing it," Sophie explained, and using a laser pointer, she circled one reference point on the screen.

"The program looked at location data where Roberts disappeared but couldn't determine if Konijn had been in that area," she said, and then moved on to another reference point.

"A review of text and other messages got a very high rank, which tells me not all was right in the world between Konijn and Roberts," Sophie said.

"There are issues between Roberts and Konijn's father. That was obvious from our interview, and it's why we added him as a suspect," Gabriella advised. She added a note beneath Ralph Konijn's name on their murder board.

Sophie drilled down another level in the data about the text messages, and Diego didn't fail to miss the line item about violent tendencies. Pointing to that, he said, "Am I reading that right? The program is predicting possible violent behavior? How does it know?"

Robbie jumped in with an explanation. "Wilson has recently been working on adding more artificial intelligence to his program. The AI has been trained to pick up on certain patterns and actions to predict human behavior."

"For real?" Diego said, both dubious and worried about the implications of programs with such power.

"For real. Researchers at MIT have created similar algorithms, and there are already programs that can review materials to diagnose schizophrenia," Sophie advised.

"If they can do that, can they predict if someone can become a serial killer?" Gabriella asked.

"Possibly. And on that note..." Sophie flipped through several screens to display one that drew a gasp and surprise from Gabriella.

"The program says there's a 95 percent probability all three disappearances are the work of a serial killer," she said, reading aloud the program's prediction.

"Looks like you were right about this, Gabby. I should have trusted your gut," Ryder said, apology alive in his tone.

A second later, Sophie hauled up another screen that elicited shocked silence from all until Sophie said, "According to the program, there's a high probability these three other cases are also connected to the serial killer."

Diego scanned the names on the screen, and one jumped out at him.

"Isabella Ruiz? Is she a relation?" he said, and glanced at Gabriella.

Her face had paled to a sickly green and in a tremulous voice, she said, "I was hoping my sister might still be alive somewhere."

A second later, she plopped heavily into the chair next to him, body shaking as she buried her head in her hands and sobbed.

He muttered a curse and wrapped an arm around Gabriella, hauling her close as he glared at Sophie and said, "You could have given her some warning."

"I didn't read the details to see the names. I'm so sorry, Gabriella," she said, and hurried over to embrace her.

Gabriella raised her head and shakily swiped tears from her face. "It's okay," she said. But Diego didn't know how that was possible.

She'd just discovered that her sister was the likely victim of a serial killer.

And he'd just learned the reason for that sadness he'd seen in her eyes.

"Maybe we should take a break. Give Gabriella a moment," he said as he squeezed her upper arm again, offering comfort.

"No. Every minute we waste is a minute less for Jeannie Roberts."

"Are you sure?" Sophie asked, gaze narrowed with worry.

"I'm sure," she said. Beneath his arm, strength flooded her body. She straightened her shoulders and grabbed a nearby pen as if to take notes on her pad.

He didn't miss the slight tremble in her hand that said she was fighting to keep it together.

"Do we have full details on those other victims' cases?" Ryder said, trying to move past the difficult moment.

Sophie shook her head. "We don't. The connections for these cases likely came from assorted police reports and possibly even true crime websites."

"It may take time to get the reports from local police," Gabriella said with a disappointed sigh.

Robbie mimicked typing with his fingers. "I could speed that up."

"Meaning?" Diego said with an arch of a dark brow.

Ryder held his hand up to stop Robbie from answering. "You don't want to know, Diego. But like Gabriella said, every minute counts."

"I should go to my office to get that info for you," Robbie said, shot to his feet and hurried from the room.

"Better we don't know how he gets it?" Diego asked, peering from Ryder to Sophie.

"He won't do anything to compromise the case. Trust us," Sophie said.

Diego hadn't worked long enough with them to trust them, but if his old friend Jackson did, he had to temper his concerns. Especially if it meant finding Jeannie Roberts and closure for Gabriella and her family.

"I trust you," Gabriella said, and he echoed her comment.

"Okay, let's dive through all this other info," Sophie said.

GABRIELLA FORCED HER mind from the moment Isabella's name had appeared on the screen, and her reaction, to the data that Wilson's program had snared from various sources on the internet.

There was so much data that Ryder had slipped from the room to bring in another whiteboard for the new victims and their information.

As they reviewed the details and listed the relevant points connecting the women, one thing was clear: Isabella didn't fit in.

She hadn't gone to the University of Denver. She hadn't been a hiker. She wasn't in the age range.

"Isabella was the first, and he probably hadn't intended to kill her," she whispered as Ryder jotted down the last bit of information from Wilson's reports.

Ryder stepped back from the board, jammed his hands on his hips and reviewed the information again before he finally said, "Yes. That's the most likely reasoning."

"Like Dahmer's first kill. That might also explain the gap until the next murder," Gabriella said, stood and walked to the murder board.

"Something made him take Isabella. He accidentally killed her, but he liked it. As for the gap, he didn't have the right opportunity to take another woman," she said, and tapped on a name on the murder board. "The opportunity came twice over the next two years. But his method was different, and judging from the gap, he didn't like something about those kills."

"They were too fast," Diego tossed out for consideration.

Gabriella couldn't disagree. She walked back to her sister's name on the board and said, "When Isabella disappeared, the area was thoroughly searched. We never found her. Same for

Cornerstone and Nations. Now we have Roberts. He likes to take time with his victims."

"Time he didn't have with those two other kills," Ryder said as he stood beside her, examining the board.

"If time is what he wants, Roberts may still be alive," Sophie said, and displayed another screen from Wilson's report.

She used the laser pointer to highlight the names of the current suspects. "We have these three. And now we've added Ralph Konijn. But according to Wilson, there are at least six other men with possible connections to our victims."

A tap came at the door a second before Robbie rushed in, laptop in hand. He paused to glance at the board before he said, "I've got info for you. I'm printing copies of all the reports for you also, but I see you have some of the names up on that list."

Which had Gabriella sighing with disgust. "So many names."

Robbie approached the monitor with the list and circled three of the names. "You can take these off the list. All these men were interviewed and had solid alibis."

"So that adds only two other names to our list," Diego said, and shuffled around some papers to read the profiles of the two new suspects. After a quick look, he said, "Both of the men are white and twenty-five. That would make them, or any of these others, only a teen at the time of Isabella's murder."

With a wave of her hand, Gabriella gestured to the file she had provided to Diego earlier that day. "When you get a chance, look at my research. In the US, our youngest serial killer was thirteen. Murdered four women including two young girls. The next oldest was seventeen. He killed three women that he stalked and murdered during home invasions."

A stunned silence filled the room, and Gabriella understood. She'd been hard-pressed to understand how someone so young could commit such heinous crimes.

"Hard to imagine, but many serial killers experience abuse at an early age," she said, and waved her hands to shut down their expected comments. "It doesn't excuse what they do, but it could explain it."

"How does it account for either of the Konijn men? I don't see either of them as being abused," Diego said.

"The father was rather domineering. Mother is likely emotionally absent. That could create the kind of environment which produces a serial killer." Gabriella paused, glanced at the board and added, "We should interview the mom."

"I agree, and if you don't mind, before we get to those police reports, I need to take Poppy for a walk," Diego said, slowly rose and stretched out a kink.

Gabriella nodded. "I think a break makes sense. I could use some fresh air as well. Do you mind if I come with?"

Chapter Nine

"Not at all," he said, grabbed his jacket from the back of his chair and slipped it on. Bending, he rubbed Poppy's head and snagged her leash. "Come on, Poppy."

He waited until Gabriella retrieved her coat and together they walked to the elevator. As they stood there, he peered at her from the corner of his eye, wondering how she was handling the fact that her missing sister might have been the victim of a serial killer.

Her arms were wrapped around herself and her face was downturned, as if she was deep in thought.

Poppy, apparently picking up on her distress, surprised him by rubbing her head against Gabriella's thigh.

With a startled jump, Gabriella came out of her thoughts. It seemed like she was about to rub Poppy's head but stopped and looked up at him.

"Is it okay?" she asked, dark eyes wide with surprise and sadness. Now he knew the reason for it.

While it wasn't normally okay to treat Poppy as if she were a pet, Gabriella seemed to need the emotional support and she was, for the moment, his partner in this investigation.

"Sure."

She rubbed Poppy's head, a shadow of a smile on her face.

A second later, the elevator arrived, they boarded and stood there in silence for a moment before Gabriella said, "Thank you."

He met her gaze, puzzled, but before he could speak, she said, "For not asking. I'm not ready to talk about it."

Nodding, he said, "I'm here when you're ready."

With a tight smile, she dipped her head in acknowledgment but remained silent.

The doors opened, and they hurried outside into the chill of the early April night.

It had grown late and the area in front of the new Crooked Pass Security office was fairly empty. But a few feet away, there was still a good amount of foot traffic in the Sixteenth Street Mall. People frequented the various hotels and restaurants that would still be open despite it being well past ten o'clock.

Diego had barely taken a step when Poppy barked and veered in the direction of the corner where someone leaned against the building close to Sixteenth Street, hood pulled low across their face. Average height. A big puffer jacket made it difficult to tell if it was a man or woman.

As the individual noticed they'd been spotted, the pair pushed off and rushed around the corner.

Poppy yanked at her leash and Diego said, "She's scented something. Let's go!"

He raced to the corner, Gabriella running beside him, and turned onto Sixteenth Street, but there was no sign of the individual.

"*Such*," he said in German, instructing Poppy to track them.

Head slightly down, as if searching for the scent, the German shepherd pulled at the leash, leading them halfway down the block and toward the doors of a nearby fast-food chain.

He jerked open the door but as they entered, there was no sign of anyone in a black hoodie and puffer jacket.

Poppy yanked him in the direction of the counter where he asked the young girl, "Did you see someone in a hoodie and puffer jacket come in?"

"Bathroom," she said, and pointed to the far side of the space.

Since Poppy was pulling them toward that area, he and Gabriella followed. At the unisex bathroom, he tried the door, but it was locked. Gabriella raced back out to the counter and returned with a key barely a minute later.

"*Setz*," he instructed Poppy, and the dog immediately sat just behind him.

He glanced at Gabriella to confirm she was ready in case the individual tried to race past them, and at her nod, he unlocked the door with the key and threw it open.

A blast of chilly air greeted them a second before they walked into the empty bathroom stall.

The individual, now a potential suspect, had climbed out the window.

They both muttered a curse at the same time and hurried back to the counter.

"Is there an entrance at the back?" Gabriella asked.

"Through the kitchen," the young woman said, and as they raced there, she called out after them, "You can't go in there!"

They pushed past teenagers assembling sandwiches to a large steel door at the back of the kitchen area.

Diego shouldered the door open and instructed Poppy to track once again. But the smells of garbage and cooking from the fast-food restaurant as well as another nearby eatery had Poppy stopping short in the narrow alley.

Too many scents and smells, he thought as he peered down the alley, trying to figure out which way their suspect might have gone.

"He could have gone in either direction," Gabriella said as she too scoped out the alley.

Gesturing to one end, he said, "That leads to Sixteenth Street. If he went that way, we might have eyes on him from any of the CCTVs in the area."

Glancing in the other direction, Gabriella said, "My money's on him going to Fifteenth and the park. Maybe doubling back to the Civic Center Station. He could hop on a bus to anywhere there."

"I agree. Let's see if Poppy can pick up the scent again," he said.

They ran to the end of the alley and popped out on Fifteenth Street.

Diego commanded Poppy to track, but after sniffing around the alley exit and then back and forth several yards in either direction, it was apparent that it would do no good.

With a frustrated sigh and shake of his head, he said, "We can head to the station, but I suspect he'll be long gone."

"I agree. Let's head back to the CPS offices and see if they can find something on him from the CCTVs."

Turning toward the Civic Center Station, they returned to the offices and as they walked, Diego said, "How do you know it's a he?"

"Most serial killers are male," she answered without hesitation.

"Isn't it dangerous to make that kind of assumption?" he said as they stopped to let Poppy relieve herself, the original reason for their walk.

She nodded. "It is. The assumption that serial killers are usually white is what delayed the capture of the Atlanta child murderer. But we have to start somewhere."

It was as good a place as any to start, he thought as he picked up after Poppy and they returned to the CPS offices.

GABRIELLA ENTERED THE conference room and found that in their absence, Sophie, Robbie and Ryder had added information beneath the photos of their original suspects and the two new names.

But her gut was telling her it had to be one of the three original suspects. Walking up to the board, she tapped on their names and said, "Diego and I just chased down someone downstairs.

Someone who Poppy recognized as having Roberts's scent. Neither of these two men even know we exist."

"Are you sure?" Sophie asked.

"Neither Gabriella nor I have spoken publicly about the case, and I don't believe our names were made available to the press, but I can check on that," Ryder said, picked up his cell phone and stepped out of the room to make the necessary calls.

"Is it possible for you to get video feeds from the area adjacent to this building on Fifteenth and Sixteenth?" Gabriella asked.

Sophie nodded. "We can check for CCTV and other feeds. What are we looking for?"

"Black puffer jacket, hoodie and jeans. Hiking boots, I think. Between five feet eight and six feet," Diego said.

"We'll get on it," Robbie confirmed, and started tapping away on his laptop.

"Great, and thanks. Which leaves us with the original three, and my gut is on the Konijn men," she said, and circled some new info that seemed rather damning. "No cell phone records at the time of Roberts's disappearance."

"We think that's suspicious as well. It warrants checking with their carriers again," Robbie said, picked up a report from the table and walked over to her with it. "These are the records the carriers gave to local law enforcement."

"It's either a glitch or intentional. My money is on intentional," Diego said as he looked at his copy of the report.

"Mine, too. The odds seem low that both of them went radio silent at the same time due to a glitch," Gabriella said, and rapped on the board with her knuckle again. "Plus, Poppy picked up a scent on Ralph. Not likely a transfer of a scent, right?" she said, and peered at Diego.

"Unlikely," he confirmed with a dip of his head.

Ryder marched back into the room, his face mottled with red and white, and set into a glower.

"Not good news, I gather," Sophie said even though it was apparent from her boyfriend's features.

"Our names were provided to local law enforcement. Crooked Pass Security was also mentioned," he said, and approached the board.

He pointed to one of the new names on the board. "Sam Hughes. He's a paramedic with the new Support Team Assisted Response program that sends a paramedic and social worker with Denver PD in cases involving either mental health or substance abuse issues. As part of law enforcement, he got info," Ryder explained, picked up a marker and jotted the information beneath Hughes' name.

"He's back on the list then, but in the meantime…" she said, and glanced at her watch. "It's nearly eleven. We should probably call it a night and reconvene in the morning."

"I think that makes sense," Ryder agreed, and walked over to Sophie, who appeared hesitant to leave her computer.

"I know you and Robbie too well, mi amor. You can work when we get home. Same for you, Robbie. I'm sure Selene is waiting for you," Ryder said, and urged Sophie to her feet.

She closed her laptop and tucked it under her arm. "You're right. We'll pick this up in the morning."

Robbie did the same and echoed Ryder's comment. "Selene will be waiting. She's probably home from the recording studio by now."

Gabriella had almost forgotten that Robbie was now involved with Selene Reilly, a rising star who had been signed by one of the country's hottest record producers and a personal favorite.

"I can't wait to hear her new album," she said with a bit of fangirl in her voice.

Robbie smiled and said, "When we find Roberts, we'll celebrate by going to her next show."

"I'd like that," she said, pleased he'd said "when" and not "if."

The crew headed down to the street where Robbie peeled off to walk to the nearby condo where he lived with Selene.

She walked with Ryder, Sophie and Diego into the underground parking lot for the building. After Ryder and Sophie said their goodbyes by one car, Diego continued walking with her.

"Is your car nearby?" she asked, and stopped next to her vehicle.

He jerked a thumb back in the direction of where Ryder and Sophie were pulling out of the parking garage. "It's in a tenant spot. I couldn't let you walk to your car alone now that we know the killer may have eyes on you."

She narrowed her gaze and considered him. "I can take care of myself," she warned.

"I have a feeling Jeannie Roberts thought the same thing, and since you fit his profile of athletic, brunette and beautiful, there's no sense taking a chance."

A rush of heat swept to her face, and she tried to tell herself that it wasn't because this very handsome man thought she was attractive. Forcing herself to ignore his comment, she said, "I'll see you in the morning."

He grinned, started to walk away, but then turned to say, "Don't stay up too late working."

She had noticed him gathering up all the reports as well and didn't doubt he'd be burning the midnight oil as well. Who wouldn't be when a woman's life was on the line?

Which had her suddenly and unexpectedly asking, "Do you want to go over the materials together?"

Chapter Ten

Stupid, stupid, stupid.

He should have been more careful.

He should have made sure not to be seen.

As it was, he'd barely been able to get away but not without a price, he thought, and grimaced. He had wrenched his back when he'd had to wriggle through the bathroom window of the fast-food chain.

But he knew just what would make him feel better.

He shifted away the chair and then the rug that hid the trapdoor into the root cellar, ignoring the pain as he lifted the door.

Taking a step down the stairs, he hit a switch, and the lights snapped on, bathing her body in glorious, cleansing brightness.

She jumped awake, that delightful fear in her eyes followed by the even more delicious eruption of courage. Her spine straightened, and she lifted her chin in challenge.

His body awoke powerfully at that, but another need rose even more powerfully.

He had to drive that spirit out of her. That was the only way to make himself whole.

He had to have control over her. Control he lacked in his own life.

As he reached the cellar floor, he looked toward the shelf where he kept his camera. Beside it was a riding crop he'd had since the first day he'd gotten up on a horse.

His father had taught him how to use it. When to use it.

His father had also used it on him to keep him in line. To make sure he did what he was told when he was told.

Just like she would stay in line tonight, he thought, and reached for the crop.

Diego had slept on far more uncomfortable surfaces during his time in the military.

Despite that, he'd probably slept better on those hard dirt and rocks than on the bed in Gabriella's guest room.

They'd stopped going over her research notes and Wilson's assorted reports at close to three in the morning. They'd forced themselves to stop only because they knew they needed rest to be sharp during that day's investigations.

She'd offered to drive him home or back to the office, but he hadn't wanted her driving around alone. Especially so late at night. Plus, he kept a spare set of clothes in his Jeep, and there was a small but serviceable washroom at the office.

His gut told him that the man who had been watching them earlier was likely the killer. And the fact that he'd been there, watching for her, worried him.

Diego didn't know what serial killer phase that might fall into. But he suspected the killer had set his sights on Gabriella. After all, what could be more tempting than to grab the sister of the girl who had been your first kill?

Those thoughts had plagued his sleep along with so many questions, chief among them: Where had the killer left the bodies of the three original missing women?

Based on what little information he'd gotten from Gabriella's research, he was sure they were all buried close together. And if they could narrow the list of locations where that might be, maybe Poppy, with her excellent sense of smell, could find them.

The whoosh of water through pipes warned that she was awake and in the shower.

Which led to the second reason for his troubled sleep.

Gabriella.

She'd been on his mind off and on during his restless night, and it wasn't just because of the investigation. He found her way too attractive, and that could only lead to problems if he lost his objectivity.

It was already difficult for him to keep from the emotional connection because of her loss.

He, possibly more than many, understood loss.

He'd suffered it way too often during his time in the military and regrettably, after.

PTSD had nearly taken his life in the many months after he'd left the Marines. With the help of friends like Jackson, he'd managed to gain the control necessary to put his life back on track. The therapy dog he'd had before Poppy had opened a new world to him, leading to his work with other veterans and a new career as a dog handler.

Poppy, he thought, and sat up to find his K-9 partner snoring peacefully by the side of the bed. Sensing his movement, Poppy awoke with a big yawn.

"Good girl," he said, and rubbed her head. Reaching for his backpack, he hauled out the emergency rations kit he always carried with him.

With a hand command, he instructed Poppy to follow him to the spacious kitchen just off the guest bedroom where he'd slept.

Uncollapsing two silicone bowls, he emptied a small plastic bag of kibble into one and filled the other with water.

Poppy immediately buried her head in the kibble bowl and wolfed down the food in record time before taking several big gulps of water.

He always wondered how she could eat so fast without any apparent signs of stomach upset.

But as Poppy glanced up at him with a happy dog grin, he shrugged and playfully rubbed her around the head and neck, which she loved. After, he cleaned the portable bowls and packed them up.

The rushing sound of water stopped and snared his attention. He forced himself not to think about Gabriella drying off in the bathroom.

Epic fail, he thought as his body responded.

Muttering a curse, he decided to make coffee to take his mind off the attractive CBI agent.

Much like her office, Gabriella's kitchen was organized with the coffeepot and coffee-making materials neatly laid out on the counter. Canisters beside the coffee pot held ground coffee and filters. A smaller canister had packets of sugar and artificial sweetener.

She was a sugar girl, he recalled from a coffee she'd made herself the night before.

Was the artificial sweetener for a boyfriend or just regular visitors? he wondered as he prepped the drip coffee maker and then pushed the button to start the brewing.

The snick of a door opening dragged his attention and Poppy's to the area behind the kitchen.

Gabriella exited her bedroom, dressed in the apparently requisite white shirt and a black pantsuit with faint gray pinstripes. Serviceable penny loafers had replaced the sexy heels she'd been wearing the day before.

It made sense, especially considering last night's chase. He'd been surprised that she'd been able to keep up with him in those heels, but somehow she had.

"Good morning," she said as she walked over and smiled at the sight of coffee dripping into the carafe. "Thanks. I think we're going to need the caffeine today."

"Good morning, and yes, we're going to need the boost after our late night," he said, and wondered why that sounded way more intimate than it had been.

She grabbed a to-go cup from a nearby cabinet and faced him with a puzzled look, possibly picking up on that.

"It was a productive night. Your research gave me a lot of insights," he said as she handed him another takeaway mug.

"I'm glad I could help," she said as she pulled off the coffee and poured it into their cups. She handed him his cup, and he waited while she prepped hers. Once she was done, she said, "Can I make you something to eat? I only usually grab something at the deli by the office."

"No, thanks. Robbie and Sophie usually bring in pastries and other goodies," he explained as he sipped his black coffee.

"I guess we should get going then. We'll have a lot to do today if we want to find Roberts alive," she said, and bolted for her front door.

He followed, but as they neared the door, he swung his arm out to keep her back. At her questioning glance, he said, "He knew where you were last night. I don't think you were followed, but we can't take a chance."

GABRIELLA HATED THAT he was right.

She was used to being her own woman, but if the serial killer had turned his attention to her, it would be dangerous to work with Diego and the rest of the team.

Diego, she thought as he slipped past her with Poppy and scoped out the grounds in front of her home.

She didn't know what to make of the handsome marine.

There was a connection between them. Attraction, possibly only physical. She couldn't deny that.

She wrote it off, chalking it up to the fact that she'd been so busy with her career and her single-minded quest to find her sister that she hadn't dated in way too long.

That was why he intrigued her, she told herself. Only as she followed his broad-shouldered and muscular body out the door and to her car at the curb, she knew it was a lie.

It was way more than that. Emotional, for sure. He seemed to understand her sense of loss more than anyone else before. Maybe because as a marine who'd been deployed to some of the world's worst war zones, he'd known loss.

When they reached her car, he did a sweep around it, letting Poppy sniff all around before declaring they were good to go.

She didn't know what he'd expected to find. A bomb maybe? Although she didn't think Poppy was trained for that.

As he sat beside her after harnessing Poppy, he said, "We should have either Robbie or Sophie check to see if anyone put a tracker on the car."

"Got it. If he's fixating on me now, we need to know what he'll do," she said as she pulled away for the trip from her home to the CPS offices in downtown Denver.

She remained on high alert as she drove, vigilant for signs that they were being followed.

With a glance in Diego's direction, he was doing the same, his gaze skipping all around to make sure they were safe.

They were about halfway to the CPS offices when she noticed a gray Range Rover in her rearview mirror. She'd spotted it at least twice before, once as they turned Wadsworth Boulevard onto Sixth Avenue and then again when she'd made the left onto North Lincoln.

"A Range Rover is giving me some worry. I'm going to let them pass," she said.

"I'll check out the driver and get the plate number," Diego said, shifting slightly in his seat to get a better look.

Gabriella slipped into the right lane and slowed, making believe she was looking for parking. The Range Rover blew past her and kept traveling up North Lincoln.

"Did you see the driver? Get the plate number?" she asked, and increased her speed for the last few turns to reach the CPS offices.

"Windows were too tinted, but I got a photo of the plate. He had one of those stealth license plate covers on," Diego said, and swiped his phone. "Robbie or Sophie may be able to work their magic on the photo."

"Good. It's probably nothing but—"

"Better safe than sorry," he finished for her.

She smiled and nodded. "Better safe than sorry."

A little over a mile later, she turned into the underground garage at the CPS offices. Since it was early, there was a spot not far from the spaces reserved for the CPS staff members.

"Is this your car?" she asked as she pulled next to a late-model khaki-colored Jeep Wrangler.

"It is. I just need to get some things from the back," he said, pulled out his keys and unlocked the Jeep.

She slipped out of the car and reached into the back seat for her briefcase with all the case materials while Diego unharnessed Poppy, grabbed his knapsack and hurried to his car.

As she walked around to the back of the Jeep, he grabbed a large black backpack with his name emblazoned on the face of it. A metal water bottle was tucked into a side pouch.

He slung that backpack over one shoulder and the smaller knapsack from the night before over the other. Leash in hand, he did a soft click with his tongue, and Poppy came to her feet for the walk to the offices.

"Robbie doesn't drive to work, I assume?" she said as they boarded the elevator.

"The condo he shares with Selene is about two blocks away. He parks a car here, but usually walks," he explained.

The elevator stopped, and the doors opened onto the floor that CPS shared with a boutique law firm.

The reception desk was empty, much as it had been the day before. "Do you have a receptionist? I didn't notice one yesterday."

"Not yet. The agency only opened its doors about a month

ago and is still working on staffing," Diego said as he badged them in.

"And clients, I assume?" she asked, wondering if that was why CPS was so willing to help on this case. Besides the obvious relationship between Sophie and her partner Ryder.

"Clients, too. They'll come in time, I suppose," he said with a nonchalant shrug.

At her questioning glance, he explained. "I'm told that they're well funded. Personal money and the backing of the Miami cousins from South Beach Security."

"They're doing this pro bono?" she asked as they walked into the conference room. She opened her briefcase to extract her files and research.

With another shrug of those wide shoulders, he said, "You might say that. But I suspect that it would help their reputation if they help you find and stop this serial killer."

She did not doubt that. For the moment, the press only knew that the CBI was investigating Roberts's disappearance. If word got out about a possible serial killer, the press would be all over it and anyone involved, including Crooked Pass Security.

The sound of the office entrance lock and footsteps drew her attention to the conference room door.

Seconds later, Sophie and Ryder strolled in arm in arm. Sophie carried a big bag from a nearby bakery, and the aroma of yeasty bread escaped into the air.

Robbie slipped in behind them carrying a large take-out jug of coffee and a smaller bag.

The siblings immediately got to work laying out an assortment of pastries and the fixings for coffee.

Gabriella's stomach growled noisily from the delicious smells, and she instantly covered it with her hand. "Sorry," she said with a laugh.

"I guess I'm not the only bottomless pit," Robbie kidded,

and winked at her playfully as he loaded a croissant and Danish onto his plate.

"Leave some for the rest of us," Diego teased, walked over and laid a hand on the small of her back.

The feel of his hand roused a mix of emotions as he often did. But her focus had to be on the case and only the case.

The clock was ticking, and she worried that time was running out for Jeannie Roberts.

Because of that, she quickly grabbed some food, refilled her coffee mug and returned to the table.

The others did as well, sensing as she did that time wasn't on their side.

"We think someone followed us this morning in a gray Range Rover. Diego got a photo of the plate that we're hoping you can enhance," she said to start the discussion.

"Send it over and we'll track it down," Sophie said.

"Great. I'd love to know if the Konijns own anything like that," Diego added.

"Easy enough to do. I'll reach out to DMV for a list of any vehicles registered to them either personally or through their company," Ryder said, and jotted down a note on a pad.

"Great. I'd like to visit the Konijns again this morning and question them about their cell phones," she said, but Ryder immediately nixed that idea.

"I'd like to see what Sophie and Robbie can find out from the carriers first. Plus, I'd like to get a read on them myself."

She hesitated, unsure, but then dipped her head in agreement. "It would be good to get your opinion on their behavior. Which I guess means it's Sam Hughes for me."

"For us. I'm not letting you go anywhere without me," Ryder said, his tone brooking no disagreement.

His assertion of control angered her. "I'm a big girl. I can take care of myself," she repeated.

"I DON'T DOUBT THAT, but I'd feel better if you had backup. Especially since someone might be tracking you. Speaking of that..." Diego paused and glanced in Sophie and Robbie's direction.

"I assume you can check if there's a tracker on Gabriella's car."

"If someone wants to follow her, they're most likely using a GPS tracker that transmits her position in real time. We have a device that can pick up that signal," Robbie said without hesitation.

"And that means they're paying for a service to carry those GPS signals. Once we locate the tracker and get its make and serial number, we should be able to find a carrier. But we'll need a warrant to find out who's paying for the service," Sophie advised.

Ryder's gaze skipped across everyone at the table as he said, "Given that they're tracking a CBI agent during an open investigation, I'm pretty sure a judge would grant that warrant."

"Can you check before we go our separate ways?" Diego asked.

Sophie nodded but with a quick few taps of her keys, she brought up some images on the monitor on the wall. "I found CCTV footage from last night. I isolated images of the individual you chased and ran programs to get basic info."

"Like what?" Gabriella asked, dark brows narrowed in question.

"Our unsub is between five feet ten and six foot. Approximate weight is hard because of the puffer jacket, but adjusting for that, between one hundred fifty and one hundred seventy-five pounds. The average height and weight for an American man," Sophie advised with an exasperated sigh.

"Which fits either of the Konijn men," Gabriella tossed out, her frustration obvious.

"Or Sam Hughes. He's six feet tall," Diego added as he

flipped through a police report that included DMV records for their possible suspect.

"*If* any of them is our unsub and *if* this is a serial killer, I'm worried about getting tunnel vision and missing the bigger picture," Ryder said, and spread some of the papers across the surface of the table. "We have three other possible suspects. We can't ignore them."

"No, we can't," Gabriella urged.

Diego could tell that this argument was one the partners had been having for some time. And he understood Ryder's reticence, since there were such differences in the way the five women identified had been either killed or taken. But he'd also picked up something from Gabriella's research and the reading he'd done the night before.

"You're concerned that the three missing women and Roberts's disappearance aren't connected. Same for those two other women. Am I right?" Diego pressed Ryder.

"Yes. The methods and opportunities are all different," Ryder said, and flipped through the papers on the desk to read out the information.

"Isabella was twelve when she was taken. The other women are all older. These two were raped and killed in their own homes," Ryder pointed out, furiously flipping through the papers in his file.

"The Night Stalker repeatedly changed MOs. He raped some. Raped and murdered others. Burglaries only in some cases. Different methods of killing for many of the victims," Diego pointed out.

Ryder leaned back in his chair, ran a hand through his hair, and glanced between him and Gabriella. "You've read Gabby's research and you're right. Different MOs don't mean it's not the same person."

"I understand your concerns, Ryder. You're right that we can't let ourselves focus on one theory so hard that we ignore other clues and suspects," Diego said, acknowledging the other man's worries.

"We'll revisit the possibility that someone besides the Konijns is responsible," Gabriella said, also trying to defuse the situation.

With a relieved sigh, Ryder nodded. "That's all I'm asking, that we keep open minds. Because we're running out of time."

"Great. Our first step is to find out if there is a tracker and start running that info," Sophie said, laying a hand on Ryder's and giving a reassuring squeeze.

"Let's go," Ryder said, and shot to his feet.

Diego rose more slowly and said, "If you don't mind, I'm going to grab a quick shower and change while you're checking Gabriella's car."

"You go ahead, Diego. The four of us can handle this for now," Robbie said.

"I won't be long," he said, stood and with a quick hand command to Poppy, who had been patiently lying by his feet, he grabbed his larger black knapsack and hurried from the room.

GABRIELLA WATCHED HIM GO, grateful for his support as well as his ability to defuse the situation with her partner. Alphas like Ryder, and Diego as well, could sometimes butt heads like two rams in heat.

But Ryder was right, as much as she might not want to admit it.

She could not let tunnel vision prevent her from saving Jeannie Roberts.

That had to be the primary objective at this moment. And if it turned out that her hunch about the serial killer and Wilson's confirmation of that was accurate, and somehow connected to Roberts's disappearance, they'd deal with that.

But first, the possible tracker, she thought as she followed Sophie, Ryder and Robbie from the room.

As they walked down the hall, Robbie ducked into his office and then returned with a small handheld device, not much bigger than a walkie-talkie. It had what looked like one fixed antenna and a longer, more flexible one.

"Is that the GPS detector?" she asked, and he nodded.

"It's nothing fancy. It just picks up RF, wireless, Bluetooth or other similar signals," he explained as they walked out of the office and to the elevators.

"If there is a tracker on the car, how would he know which one was mine unless…" She paused, recalling all the locations she'd been the day before and whether anyone had had the time to plant the device.

"Unless it was one of the people you visited yesterday," Ryder finished for her.

"Seems unlikely, but I'm keeping all possibilities open. If Sam Hughes got word early in the day about us and CPS, he could have been here watching," she said, wanting Ryder to know that she had taken his concerns to heart.

Ryder offered her a half smile and dipped his head as they exited the elevators on the parking level and walked toward Gabriella's car.

When they were standing beside it, Robbie flipped on the GPS detector and as if to prove to her how it worked, he said, "Hold out your phone."

She did as he asked, and he ran the fixed antenna over it. A meter on the device jumped to life, the lights zipping upward into the red level.

"That's what it'll look like if we get a hit," he said, and then unraveled the flexible antenna that had a small LED light at the end.

"Most likely place is the wheel well," he said, and ran the hard antenna all around before inserting the flexible end beneath her driver-side rear wheel well.

"The flexible one detects if a magnet is holding the GPS tracker in the well," he said as he scanned, but nothing registered.

He repeated those actions at the front wheel well and then walked around to the other side.

No hits on either of those, but as he approached the back

passenger wheel, the first little blip sounded at one spot, and the lights and bleeping went off the chart.

"We've got a hit," he said, and flipped some kind of switch on the device. He inserted the flexible antenna and as he ran it across one area, the lights and sound jumped high.

He reached underneath, scrabbled beneath the edge and then pulled out a small black box.

Both Sophie and he muttered a curse as they looked at the tracker.

"What's wrong?" she asked.

"It's a cheap tracker you can buy at several stores. The user has to insert their own SIM card to get it to operate," Sophie explained.

Robbie tacked on, "We'll have to open it and inspect the SIM to find the carrier. The signal will be interrupted, which may tip them to the fact that we found it."

Gabriella shook her head and glanced all around the parking lot. "How accurate is it? I mean, does someone know if the tracker is here or up in your offices?"

With a shrug, Robbie said, "One like this might not know the difference."

"I'll take another car to see Hughes while the two of you try to find out more," Gabriella said.

"That sounds like a plan. Call me as soon as you know the carrier and I'll reach out for that warrant," Ryder said, bent and dropped a kiss on Sophie's temple. "I'll interview the Konijns, father and son. If I have time, I'll also fit in Baxter and Kinston just to be sure I'm getting the same read as you did."

"We'll meet back here to see what other info Robbie and Sophie have, plus anything else that Wilson may have come up with about the connections between all our suspects," Gabriella said.

"Agreed," Ryder said, and peeled away to go his car while

she went with Sophie and Robbie to return to their office and reunite with Diego.

Diego, she thought, and ignored that little race of her heartbeat as she anticipated seeing him again.

When they entered the CPS office, she noticed Poppy lying by a door at the end of the hall and walked toward the German shepherd.

The dog raised her head at her approach and gave her what she interpreted as a happy doggy grin. She went to rub the dog's head but then pulled her hand back, conscious of Poppy's role as a working dog.

A second later, Diego jerked open the door while pulling down a black T-shirt. For a hot second, she caught a glimpse of his hard body and a network of scars along his ribs.

His chocolate-colored hair was damp and bore evidence of being finger-combed. The slight stubble that had been on his face that morning had been shaved clean, exposing the sculpted lines of his face. She noticed then another set of fine lines by his jaw, close to his earlobe.

"Everything okay?" he asked at her too-long perusal.

"N-n-no. Robbie found a tracker. We're leaving my car here so they can examine the SIM card without alerting whoever is tracking us," she said with a slight stammer and the heat of an embarrassed flush.

With a boyish grin, Diego finished tugging his T-shirt into place and said, "Whenever you want to go."

"Right now would be good," she said, and whirled away to hide her reaction.

DIEGO TOLD HIMSELF not to feel satisfaction that the attraction wasn't one-sided. He told himself it was only physical. Except it wasn't.

He admired her intelligence and her determination. He understood her loss, which roused all kinds of emotions deep in his gut. He'd learned how to deal with his own pain, although it hadn't been an easy path to find a small measure of peace.

He hoped that besides finding out the truth about what had happened to her sister, she could heal as well.

As she walked down the hall, he commanded Poppy to follow and detoured to his office to pick up the smaller knapsack that he'd restocked in case Poppy needed food or water while they were on the road. Slipping on his jacket, he grabbed the knapsack and met Gabriella, who was waiting by the elevator.

She hit the call button as he approached and since it was early, the elevator reached them quickly.

They stood beside each other silently, avoiding the obvious attraction between them.

Down in the parking garage, they exited only to find that Robbie was running the GPS tracking device over Diego's car.

As they approached, he said, "Didn't want to take any chances. It's clean...for now. Sophie is working on the SIM to find out who's the carrier."

"Thanks. We'll keep you posted if we need anything else after we talk to Hughes," Diego said, and unlocked his Jeep.

He let Gabriella pass first and then opened the rear door to let Poppy hop up. Once she was seated, he harnessed her to keep her safe as they drove and then hurried over to the driver's seat.

He started the car, tapped on the navigation button, and Gabriella read off Hughes's address, which he entered into the system. Hughes's home address in the Denver suburb of Centennial was only about twenty minutes away. He chuckled because it seemed like everywhere he ever wanted to go took only twenty minutes.

"What's so funny?" she asked as he pulled onto West Colfax to access the entrance to the highway.

"It seems like everything in the suburbs is always twenty minutes away. I'm still not used to that," he said with a shake of his head as he hit the accelerator to reach highway speed.

"Why is that? Where did you grow up?" she asked with a side-eyed glance.

"My parents raised exotic plants and orchids on a farm on the edges of the Everglades. Nothing was ever just twenty minutes away," he said with another chuckle.

"That must have been a very different experience growing up."

"It was. I learned to be self-sufficient. And there were rough spots at times when weather damaged the greenhouses and plants. It's why I went the ROTC route," he explained as they sped along the highway.

"Where did you grow up?" he said, and peeked in her direction.

With a full-lipped, happy smile, she said, "About twenty minutes outside Denver. My dad was an accountant. My mom taught at our local elementary school. It was a fairly normal life until…"

He didn't need to hear what the until was, and another quick look in her direction confirmed that sadness had filled her features yet again.

He also didn't need to hear why she'd gone into law enforcement. That was obvious.

Gabriella wanted justice for Isabella and all the other victims like her.

"My life was fairly normal, too, until I got deployed to Afghanistan. I'd never experienced anything like that. The heat. Cold. Dust everywhere always," he said, hoping that by sharing they could both heal a little more.

"That must have been very different from the Everglades," she said in commiseration.

"It was. And then there was the violence. The people hurt by terrorists who didn't care if it was us they killed or their own," he said, emotion choking his throat.

She skimmed a hand down his arm, offering comfort. "I can't imagine what that must have been like. It changes you."

"It does," he said, and shook his head before he continued, hands tight on the steering wheel as so many memories cascaded through his brain.

"It weighed on me, even after I left the Marines. And it sometimes got to be too much to handle. Thankfully I had friends like Jackson—"

"Sophie and Robbie's cousin? The police chief?" she asked.

He nodded. "He's a good friend. He helped me get into a group to deal with my PTSD. Some of the therapy was with dogs, and that led to my visiting another vet out in Idaho who was training canines."

He glanced to where Poppy was harnessed in the back seat. "It changed my life."

That comforting touch came on his arm again, and softly she said, "Thank you for sharing."

With an offhand shrug that wasn't even close to what he was feeling, he said, "Partners need to understand each other."

Chapter Eleven

Partners.

She didn't know why she liked the sound of that more than she should.

"Partners," she repeated. "But I take the lead in questioning Hughes."

"Of course. You're the cop, after all. I'm just the muscle with the dog," he said with that grin that did all kinds of things to her insides.

She suspected humor was one of the ways that he dealt with difficult situations. Many of her colleagues at the CBI did the same. It wasn't her coping mechanism. She wasn't sure she had one, come to think of it.

For too long she'd been single-mindedly doing what she needed to advance at CBI and to find out what had happened to Isabella. That hadn't left a lot of time for personal interactions other than Ryder and her other CBI colleagues.

Maybe now it was time to expand that tight circle. She got the sense that Sophie and Robbie would make good friends and allies.

As for Diego, she didn't know where that might go, she thought. She took a quick look at him as he maneuvered off the highway and onto the side streets that would take them to Hughes's home.

She had checked his schedule the night before, and he wasn't due to start an afternoon shift for several hours.

Hughes's house was in what most would consider a typical suburban housing development. Trees with the first buds of green lined the street beside nicely manicured lawns that were also beginning to show the signs of spring after last week's unseasonable snow.

She immediately noticed there were two cars in the driveway.

A Jeep like Diego's, but all black except for the bright red rims and brakes on the wheels.

Next to it was a silver-gray Range Rover.

Too much coincidence. But as they drove past the driveway to park in front of the next house, she noticed that the license plate on this car was completely legible, unlike the darkened plate on the vehicle that had followed them. It was easy enough to change out plates, she reasoned.

Diego must have read her mind. "Different plates, but that doesn't rule it out. But I think these windows aren't as tinted."

"I didn't get a good enough look at the windows to judge." She'd been too worried about the possibility that someone would either take a shot at them or try to drive them off the road. Although she'd taken defensive driving courses, there were never any guarantees if someone was truly trying to do harm.

"Let's see what Sam Hughes has to say," she said, and shut off the car.

I'M ALIVE, SHE THOUGHT as she woke to a world of hurt.

Jeannie forced herself to ignore the punishment he'd inflicted the night before.

She had no doubt that's what it was and very different from what he'd done the other two nights.

The change worried her.

He struck her as a spoiled child who would kick and scream to get what he wanted but would also lose interest quickly once he had it.

Had he lost interest in her already?

Was her time running short because of that?

Don't think about it, Jeannie. Focus, she told herself as she pulled the blanket up to her chin against the chill.

She was still alive, and he was gone for the day.

Even though it was dark in the cellar, she knew it was day because she'd heard him walking around. The noise said that he was getting ready to leave for the day.

Which meant she had hours before he would return.

Hours before he'd torture her again.

She wanted the torture, twisted as that was.

The torture meant she might live to see another day.

But she wasn't going to huddle there, praying that someone would save her.

She had to find a way to save herself.

Yanking on the chains, it seemed to her that they weren't as secure as they had been.

In the dark, she worked her fingers up the chain to where it was secured. Feeling around the eyebolt buried deep in the wall, it seemed as if the wall was crumbling.

She worked at it with her fingernail. She made more of a dent in the area around the bolt.

Was it possible? Could she scrape away enough of the wall to work the bolt loose?

But what then? There were still three other bolts.

But if she could do it with one, maybe she could do it with the others.

A fingernail wouldn't be enough to do it quickly, though, she thought.

He'd left her some food after punishing her. A tray with soft foods she could eat with the plastic spoon he thought she couldn't turn into a weapon against him.

Reaching out, she grabbed the spoon.

The bowl was too thin and fragile, but the handle was thicker. Stronger.

It would have to do, she thought as she attacked the crumbling cement.

DIEGO STOOD JUST behind Gabriella with Poppy in a position where, if necessary, he could give the attack command.

But as the door opened after Gabriella's knock, it didn't appear that would be necessary.

A petite twentysomething woman wearing the latest in yoga clothing and dabbing her sweat-damp forehead with a towel answered the door.

"May I help you?" she asked, question clouding her clear blue gaze.

Gabriella held up her CBI badge. "Is Sam Hughes available?"

"What's this about?" she said, and remained in the doorway, blocking their entry, but as she stood there, a mountain of a man came from the back of the house, a baby balanced on his hip.

"Who is it?" he called out, and walked toward the door.

The young woman finally stepped aside and as Sam Hughes neared the door, she took the baby from him and walked to one side of the living area of the home.

Sam glanced at the CBI badge as Gabriella held it up again and said, "I'm CBI Agent Gabriella Ruiz and this is my civilian consultant, Diego Rodriguez. Do you mind if we have a word with you about the disappearance of Jeannie Roberts?"

He shrugged impossibly huge shoulders that topped a heavily muscled bodybuilder's body. "Sure, but I don't know how I can help. I don't know the woman," he said, and motioned for them to enter.

As they did so, he scanned the room for any threats and to also get a feel for who Sam Hughes was.

The house screamed average, normal, middle-class family.

Not what he'd expected, since Wilson's info hadn't mentioned anything about Hughes being a father and husband.

"You were both at DU together. Both business majors," Gabriella said, but he knew that wasn't accurate and she was baiting him. Hughes had been a science major.

He immediately corrected her. "I was premed, and DU has thousands of students. Like I said before, I don't know her."

"What about Missy Cornerstone or Alyssa Nations?" she asked. At that, Hughes's body did a little twitch, and his lips thinned into a tight line.

"I was in a frat, and I'm pretty sure Missy was in a sister sorority. We might have partied together. Done some of the charity events that happen as part of Greek life," he admitted, and then quickly added, "I don't get it. What does this have to do with me?"

"Do you know Missy disappeared almost three years ago?" Gabriella pressed.

All color fled from beneath the tan on Hughes's skin. "No, I didn't. We weren't close and didn't keep in touch after college."

"Where were you on Sunday?" she asked, and Hughes glanced back at his wife, who hurried and wrapped an arm around his waist.

"He was with us. We were home watching the Rockies play the Reds. It was an afternoon game," his wife said.

"Who won?" Diego blurted out.

There was no hesitation as the duo said, almost in unison, "Rockies. Six to one."

"Is that your Range Rover in the driveway, Sam?" she asked, once again trying to elicit a deceptive response.

"No. The Jeep is mine. The Range Rover is Sara's," he said, and dipped his gaze to his wife.

"If you don't believe him, check the back seat. There's a baby seat there," Sara said, challenge and defensiveness in her voice.

"We will," Gabriella said, ice in her tone.

She reached into her jacket pocket, took out a business card and handed it to Sam. "If you can think of anything, or anyone, who might have connections to Missy and the two other women, I'd appreciate a call."

Hughes peered at the card and then nodded. "Sure. Of course. Anything to help."

"Great," she said, and Sam reached past her to open the door and let them out.

As they walked down the path to their car, Gabriella said, "What do you think?"

"Doesn't strike me as a serial killer, but then again, BTK. Family man, right?" he said, and as they walked past the Range Rover, he stopped to peer into the back. "Car seat is right where she said it would be."

Gabriella looked in as well. "Definitely a car seat. But let's note the plate number so we can get the vehicle identification number from the registration. If we need to, we'll get a warrant and ask the manufacturer to provide location data. Same with the Jeep."

Diego snapped off photos of the plates and said, "Do you mind if I walk Poppy? She needs to go, and she's not used to all this inactivity."

"Not a problem. It'll help clear my brain as well," she said and walked beside him as they strolled down the block.

The neighborhood was quiet. People were just starting to wake and get ready for school and work.

"Nice. Was your neighborhood like this growing up?" he said as he scrutinized the houses along the street. They seemed like the kind of suburban homes you'd see in movies and television shows.

Gabriella looked around and nodded. "Kind of like this. Different from the Everglades, I suspect."

"There are some small developments here and there, but it is way different from my family's home and business," he said, and stopped to pick up Poppy's waste. When he was done, he backtracked to where his Jeep was parked by Hughes's home.

There was activity in the Hughes household. Passing shadows cast on the window blinds said the couple were still inside.

"Wilson's program picked him for a reason, but I'm not feeling it," Diego said as he did a last look at the house while he harnessed Poppy into the back seat.

"Connections, I assume. The program may have picked up on their associations in college. I think I remember seeing in the report that Hughes used to be a rock climber. He might do that in the same areas as the trails where the women disappeared."

"He seems kind of muscle-bound for a rock climber," Diego said as he slipped into the driver's seat and Gabriella sat beside him.

"He does. And the man watching us last night was leaner. I'm guessing Hughes is well over two hundred pounds."

"Easily," Diego confirmed, and glanced at her. "Where do we go now? Back to CPS?"

She nodded. "Back to CPS to wait for Ryder. Hopefully, Sophie and Robbie will have more for us, and you and I can go over all this data again. See if we missed anything."

There was so much data with the information Gabriella and Ryder had gathered plus all that Wilson had provided. Maybe too much data.

He was used to being a boots-on-the-ground kind of investigator. What they were doing now felt too much like being an armchair quarterback, and he'd rather be out on the field.

Shooting a glance at his watch, he said, "I've got a better idea."

Chapter Twelve

Gabriella wasn't sure that visiting the site of her sister's disappearance was a "better idea."

She hadn't been there in a long time, and in the years since her sister had been taken, the scout camp had shut down. She suspected that what had happened to Isabella had been one of the reasons for the closure, since it was too hard to secure the area if anyone wanted to do harm.

It saddened her because she had attended the same camp years earlier and enjoyed her time there.

She slipped from the Jeep as Diego freed Poppy and then stood in the abandoned parking lot, examining the remaining trail that led into the woods and eventually, what had once been the scout camp.

He whirled on one heel and faced her. "Is this area similar to where Roberts disappeared?"

She shook her head. "No. This is a beginner trail. I know because I stayed at this camp a few years before Isabella when I was a Cadette."

"Would you mind taking me to the camp?" he asked, brow furrowed with worry since it might be difficult for her.

She sucked in a breath and held it, trying to calm the way her gut was twisting at being at the camp again. But with a resigned nod, she said, "Sure. I think I remember the way."

Liar. The way to the camp was tattooed on her brain. She'd walked it dozens of times in the weeks and months after her sister's disappearance, hoping to find something that might tell her what had happened to Isabella.

She took a halting step toward the trailhead and had to take another bracing breath. The air was colder here at the slightly higher elevation and scented with pine.

The gentle touch of his hand came at her shoulder. He squeezed reassuringly and whispered against the side of her face, "You don't have to do this if it's too hard."

It *was* too hard, but that wasn't about to stop her.

"I'm okay. I can do this," she said, but it was more to convince herself than him.

She took the first step up the trail. The ground was still hard beneath her feet but once it warmed up, it would become a slushy mess until it dried out in the warmer months.

In happier times that's when the scouts would descend on the camp to enjoy the forest and a nearby lake whose waters were fed by nearby mountain streams.

She could still remember the shocking cold after jumping in after a hot summer hike.

Diego walked a few feet behind her while Poppy sniffed the trail edges here and there, seemingly happy to be outdoors and moving around.

All around, the first signs of spring were visible, from the bright green buds on the trees to the first hints of bluebells and some errant and belated snowdrops poking their heads up from beneath the underbrush and remnants of fall leaves.

It didn't take long to reach the camp. It was a beginner's trail, after all.

There was still a clearing amid half a dozen or so wooden platforms where large canvas tents had once risen to provide shelter.

She stood in the middle of the clearing and did a slow pirouette, taking it in while Diego and Poppy walked the edges of the platforms.

Pointing to another smaller trail, she said, "There are two other platforms a little farther uphill. They're on the way to an outhouse and some shower stalls. That's where Isabella was bunking for the night."

"She wasn't alone, right?" he asked, and joined her in the center.

"No. There were three other girls in the tent. No one remembered hearing anything, but one of the girls thought that Isabella might have gone to use the bathroom," she said, recalling the witness statements that had been provided by her fellow scouts and camp counselors.

Diego walked up the narrower trail leading to the two other platforms and slightly farther away, the ramshackle remains of what must have been the toilets and showers. The wood was silvery gray from age and cracked in spots. Part of the structure had fallen in at one end, and broken wooden slats littered the ground around the building.

He let Poppy nose around the space, not that he expected the dog to get any hits. There was nothing to indicate Roberts had been here.

But something niggled at him again as it had during their discussion in the offices the day before.

Turning, he realized that Gabriella was still standing in the central clearing, arms wrapped around herself.

He returned there and raised the issue again. "I know this area was searched, as were the others, but if he keeps them for a few days, as you believe, he'd dump them after the searches were done."

Gabriella did a slow dip of her head in agreement. "I get what you're saying. But he could be dumping them anywhere."

"Bundy called his killing fields 'sacred ground,'" he said, recalling a statement he'd read while doing some research on his own.

Gabriella's nod was more emphatic this time. "Yes, he did.

The sicko even wanted his ashes scattered there after his execution."

Diego muttered a curse at the depravity of that wish but then pushed on. "What makes them special? Why does he choose that area?"

"Usually, it's a remote area. Like Gilgo Beach for LISK, but not always. Sometimes they just dump them where it's convenient and they're unlikely to be discovered."

Diego held his hands out wide. "This is a remote area. And if Isabella was his first, wouldn't this be a special area for him?"

GABRIELLA DID A slow pivot, examining the woods around them. The area was remote and since the camp had closed down a few years after Isabella's disappearance, it wasn't a commonly visited location as far as she knew. The trails were too short and easy for any hiker to want to use them.

"Possibly. But this area was used for years after Isabella was taken. If he left her here, she might have been discovered by other scouts," she said.

Diego motioned to the large hillside beyond the clearing for the tents and washroom facilities. "When you stayed here, did you ever go up to that higher ground?"

Gabriella shook her head. "Not to the top. The trails only go about halfway up the mountain, and we rarely went beyond a lake that's about one hundred yards away. We'd swim there."

Diego jammed his hands on his hips and peered up the mountainside. "That leaves a lot of ground that was possibly never searched. And the Cornerstone and Nations disappearances occurred after the camp was being used, right?"

"Right. They stopped using the camp about three years after…and it was another two years before Cornerstone disappeared," she said. She peered up the mountainside beyond the camp area.

A loud snap and crunch suddenly pulled their attention back

toward the parking lot area. They stood there, vigilant, and a minute later, a softer thud, like someone carefully closing a car door, sent them into action.

They raced down the trail at a run, hoping to see who had come to the location.

Diego stumbled on an exposed tree root and went down hard. Gabriella offered him a hand up and he scrambled to his feet, Poppy loping beside him.

As they hit the ground at the trailhead, the only car visible in the area was his Jeep.

He muttered a curse. "I'm sorry. If I hadn't fallen, we might have caught whoever that was," he said with a shake of his head.

"Don't blame yourself. We were too far away," she said, and looked his way. "You're bleeding."

He swiped at his chin, and his hand came away wet with blood. "I have a first aid kit in the back of the Jeep," he said, and used the key fob to open the hatch.

They walked there together, and he pulled up the floor to reveal a spare tire, a road kit, and beside it, a bright red first aid kit.

Gabriella grabbed the kit and once the floor was back in place, urged him to sit on the tailgate. She opened the kit and removed alcohol pads, antiseptic and a bandage to cover the cut just beneath his chin. Ripping open the alcohol pad, she said, "This is going to sting."

"I've had worse," he said, and she didn't doubt it. She'd seen the evidence that morning when she'd caught a glimpse of his scars.

Delicately she wiped the dirt away from the cut and the area around it. Luckily it was more like bad road rash than a deeper cut. "It's not that bad."

"It's not your face," he teased with that boyish grin again that made dimples erupt.

"It's not my face because I'm not clumsy," she teased right

back as she dabbed on some antiseptic and then covered the injury with a bandage.

But as she finished, something made her cup his cheek and tenderly run her thumb across the slight indent in his chin. "Thank you."

His brows narrowed in question as he said, "What for?"

"Believing in my theory. Being willing to take the extra step to find out what happened to Isabella and all those women."

A half smile ghosted across his lips before he cradled her cheek. "I want you to have closure. To see some of that sadness drift out of those beautiful eyes," he said, voice deep with emotion.

His caring stirred her. "I wish I could do the same for you. I know you've been hurt. That you still hurt and... I'm here for you if you ever want to share more," she said because he'd already told her a part of his story, but not enough for her to understand what had made him the man he was.

The smile broadened into a crooked grin. "Someday, maybe."

He slapped his hands on his thighs and said, "We should head back to CPS. I want to ask Sophie and Robbie if we can somehow use one of their fancy tech things to scope out this mountainside."

"I agree," she said, and handed him the first aid kit. He lifted the floor and returned it to its place and then followed her so he could harness Poppy in the back seat.

But as she neared the passenger door, she noticed what looked like an envelope tucked beneath the windshield wiper.

She was about to reach for it but then pulled her hand back. She stopped Diego as he also went to grab it.

"It could be evidence," she said, her gut tightening with the realization that whoever had been in the parking lot had been there for them.

She reached into her coat pocket, pulled out nitrile gloves and slipped them on.

Gently she lifted the windshield wiper and removed the small envelope.

It had her name on it in block letters and contained something small.

Hands shaking, she spilled the envelope contents into the palm of her gloved hand.

Chapter Thirteen

All color fled her face, and her body swayed, like a tower about to topple.

Diego reached out just as her knees buckled and offered support by wrapping an arm around her waist.

"What's wrong?" he asked, but then he noticed the thin gold chain and crucifix in her palm.

He didn't need to hear her say it, but her words confirmed his worst suspicions. "This was Isabella's. He left it beneath the windshield wiper," she said in a shaky voice.

"Okay. Let's get inside the Jeep where it's warmer," he said. He was worried she was in shock.

He bundled Gabriella inside the vehicle, sick with worry and guilt. If he hadn't fallen, they might have seen who had been in the parking lot.

Muttering a curse, he stepped away from the Jeep to examine the ground by the front of the Jeep where their serial killer may have stood as he placed the envelope on the windshield. He let Poppy nose around and she stopped at one spot and laid down by one of the tires.

Sure enough, there was a boot print by the front tire. He took a glove out of his pocket and placed it by the boot print to mark the evidence.

Walking to the back of the Jeep, he examined the dirt and leaves in the parking lot, Poppy walking beside him. The ground was mostly frozen, but there were patches here and there where the sun had warmed it enough to defrost. And in two of those spots were the imprints of tire treads.

He took a quick look at them and then at his tires. They weren't his, and he marked them with gloves as well.

Based on those two tire tracks, he imagined where the car might have traveled and slowly walked that area to look for any other signs of the serial killer, but there were none.

Satisfied he had preserved as much evidence as he could, he returned to the Jeep and Gabriella. With a hand command, he instructed Poppy to sit.

She was still seated there, almost zombie-like, but at least some color had returned to her face. As she noticed him, she lowered the window and mouthed, "I'm sorry."

He cradled her cheek and said, "No worries. Poppy and I have identified a boot print and some tire tracks. I'll call Ryder and see if CBI's CSI can come and make casts of them for identification."

She shook her head and whispered a strained, "No. No, I'll do it. I can't let him get into my head."

He understood. She couldn't let the serial killer be the one in control.

"Got it. I'm going to start the car so we have some heat," he said as she carefully slipped the envelope and necklace into an evidence bag.

He opened the back door and clicked his tongue so that Poppy would hop in. Once she was harnessed, he carefully walked around to make sure there were no other boot prints and climbed into the driver's seat.

Gabriella had made the call and was chatting with Ryder as he started the Jeep.

"Diego found some evidence. We need to get casts of the boot prints and tire tracks," she said, and glanced in his direction.

A mumbled response drifted across the line to which Gabriella responded, "We can't move the Jeep. It'll compromise the evidence. We'll wait for you."

She ended the call, dropped her phone into one of the cup holders, and then stared at the envelope and cross she had placed into an evidence bag. "He didn't just put a tracker on my car. He's watching us. Me."

Diego couldn't argue with that. "You're right. We need to up your protection."

She vehemently shook her head. "No. We need to let him play his game. Let him make a mistake that leads us to him."

"That'll put you in danger, and that's not acceptable," he said, but she just shook her head again and met his gaze.

"It wouldn't be the first time. And it may keep Jeannie Roberts alive longer," she said, and nervously fingered the bagged envelope and cross once again.

He reached over and stayed the anxious motion. "What if it does the opposite? What if he decides he's done with her?"

"THAT'S A POSSIBILITY," she said. She couldn't deny Diego might be right. "I just hope that by distracting him with me, he'll forget about her for a little bit. Enough for us to find her."

Or at least that's what she hoped as she set the bag with her sister's necklace and crucifix on the dashboard to keep from handling it and possibly damaging any evidence.

But with it sitting up there, the bright spring sunlight making the gold glint with life, pain jabbed her middle like a gut punch.

It was like losing her sister all over again, and she sucked in a breath and held it, trying to dam up the emotions threatening to overwhelm her.

The gentle touch of his hand on her cheek undid her, and she buried her face in her hands and let the tears come. The sobs racked her body until his arms awkwardly wrapped around her, offering comfort. He soothed her by rubbing his hands up and down her arms and murmuring words whose meaning was lost in the sea of emotions flooding her.

Slowly calm returned, and she said, "I'm okay. Really, I'm okay."

He released her, and she sat up straighter and wiped away the remnants of tears from her face. "When we're done here, I need to tell my parents."

"Whatever you need. The team can handle whatever evidence we have until you're ready," he said, and did one final stroke down her arm in sympathy.

She nodded and met his concerned gaze. "I'm ready. I have to be."

The honk of a car horn dragged her attention from Diego to Ryder's SUV as it stopped on the road leading into the parking lot. A CBI CSI van had already pulled up in front of him, and CSI techs streamed out of the car and donned jumpsuits and other protective clothing to keep them from contaminating the crime scene.

Ryder remained by his SUV, keeping free of the scene.

"We should brief him," Gabriella said, and stepped out, careful not to tread on the boot print Diego had marked.

She mindfully walked away from Diego's Jeep and to Ryder.

"You okay?" Ryder asked, concern etched onto his features as he stroked a hand down her arm.

"As well as can be expected," she said as Diego joined them.

Ryder looked at the other man and winced as he glanced at his chin. "Did he attack you?"

"No such luck. I'm just clumsy and fell as I ran down the trail and no, we didn't get a look at whoever left the…the…" he said, stumbling as he tried to describe what the killer had left.

"Evidence. His trophy," Gabriella said. As close as she was to this case, she had to remain clinical if they were going to catch him.

Ryder's dark brows shot up in question. "He left his trophy? Isn't that unusual?"

"It is but... Isabella also had half of a 'Best Friends' bracelet we got out of a cereal box. I suspect he still has that," she said, throat choking up as she thought about how she and Isabella had laughed while they'd slipped on the bracelets and vowed to never remove them. Hers was carefully tucked away in a jewelry box.

Diego's soft touch came at her shoulder, providing comfort again, and she looked up at him and offered a forced smile in thanks.

"It may be another hour or so to make the casts and dust for fingerprints," Ryder said, and peered at where the CSI agents were working in the parking lot.

"Gabriella needs to see her parents. Do you mind if we take your car? I can leave you the keys for mine," Diego said, and held his keys up to Ryder.

Ryder swiped the keys from Diego's hand and held out his keys, but as Diego took them, he met Gabriella's gaze. "Are you good with that? Would you rather I went with you?" he said, likely because they had been partners for far longer than she had known Diego.

But despite that, the connection with Diego was strong and he understood the loss she might be feeling. Again. As fresh as it had been the day Isabella had disappeared.

"I'm good with that. More than good," she said, and risked a glance at Diego, who forced a smile and squeezed her shoulder once more.

"Okay. We'll meet back at the office once you're done," he said, and didn't wait for her reply to join the CSI agents at work.

Gabriella watched him walk off and then met Diego's gaze.

"Are you sure?" he asked, clearly needing reassurance of her decision.

She smiled and cupped his cheek. "I've never been more sure."

He nodded. "Let's go then."

Chapter Fourteen

Idiot, idiot, idiot, he said to himself and cursed.

It had been impossible to stay and see her reaction to his little gift. He should have realized that and waited until the car had been somewhere else.

Somewhere he could have watched the doubt at what she was seeing become pain with the realization.

Idiot, he chastised again and opened his phone to check the location of the tracker.

Still at the Crooked Pass Security offices, which didn't surprise him since they'd used a different vehicle to go to the scout camp.

But was it just coincidental that they'd done that, or had they found the tracker?

He drove away that worry and fantasized about how she had handled his little gift. Had she cried or had she put on her tough-cop persona?

He grew hard at the thought of the latter. He loved strong women, because he loved seeing them break.

Just like Jeannie Roberts, he thought.

But then a knock came at the door, jolting him from those thoughts.

"Come in," he called out, voice gruff with lust.

"Your 2:00 p.m. meeting canceled. They said they'd reschedule," his secretary said, rousing anger at her interruption.

"You couldn't just call to tell me that," he snapped.

"I'm sorry. I just thought—"

"Well, think better next time," he said, and waved his hand in dismissal.

His secretary backed away quickly and closed the door.

He opened his computer and scanned his calendar. With his 2:00 p.m. canceled, he had the rest of the afternoon free.

He knew just what to do with all that free time.

GABRIELLA PARKED THE car in front of a brightly painted Victorian home just a block or so from Highlands Square.

"Is this where you grew up?" he asked, taking in the quaint tree-lined street populated by many other well-kept Victorians as well as some smaller bungalows and cottages.

She nodded and peered toward the home. "It is. The neighborhood has changed a little. A lot of the homes have been renovated, and the town center is more upscale than I remember. But it was a great place to grow up until…"

She didn't need to finish. It would have been great until Isabella's disappearance.

"People mean well, but it must have been hard with everyone's sympathy and helpfulness," he said, his tone a little more bitter than he intended.

She whirled to face him, eyes narrowed to examine him. "It *was* hard. You sound like you know what it's like."

He didn't normally share, but since her life and grief had been laid bare before him, he shrugged and revealed what he normally kept private.

"I lost most of my team during our last deployment. We had been sent in to raid a house where insurgents had taken several marines hostage. As we approached in the helicopter, we were hit by a rocket. The copter had to make a crash landing and many of my team members were instantly killed. Those of us that survived found ourselves under attack from the Taliban, and we lost another three people to enemy fire," he said.

Gabriella didn't say a thing. She just reached over and ran the back of her hand across his cheek before dropping it down to rest over his heart.

He covered her hand with his and braved a smile. "Thanks. If anyone understands, it's you."

She nodded and sucked in a deep breath. Her words exploded from her mouth as she said, "I don't know how to tell them."

"Do you want me to do it?" he asked, willing to shoulder the burden if it would ease her suffering.

She vehemently shook her head. "No, I need to do it. I know they were still hoping..." She stopped, muttered a curse and looked away, shaking her head again. "I can't lie. Even though I knew better, I was hoping Isabella would come home as well."

He stroked his hand over hers and said, "I get it. I can't tell you how many times I replayed that raid in my head, wondering how I could have changed what happened."

A strangled laugh escaped her. "Me, too. I ask myself why I didn't go on the overnight also. As a student counselor, I could have. But I had something else to do and I thought, 'What could happen?'"

Twining his fingers with hers, he squeezed her hand. "Maybe it's time we both stop trying to change the past and work on building a different future."

She nodded in agreement and offered him a small smile. "I'd like that but for now..."

Looking away, she said, "I have to deal with the present."

He offered another reassuring squeeze before releasing her hand so she could exit the car.

She waited for him at the curb and slipped her hand into his as they walked up the path toward the front door. Along the edges of the path, daffodils and tulips had pushed their way from the dark soil, providing bright spots of yellow, white, pink and red.

Joyful colors. Not that there would be much joy in this house today, Diego thought.

As they neared the front door, it opened, and a woman came to the door.

Gabriella's mother, he was sure. If he wanted to know what the CBI agent would look like in thirty years, all he had to do was look at the woman now standing on the front porch, arms wrapped around herself. Her gaze puzzled at first until it met her daughter's and realized this was not a happy visit.

"Javier," she called out, looking back over her shoulder. "Gabriella is here with...a friend," she said but didn't move from her spot on the front porch.

When Gabriella reached her, she laid a hand on her forearm and said, "We should go inside, Mami. I have something to tell you."

The woman's lips tightened and her face went pale, but she did as Gabriella asked, and they followed her into a large sunny parlor. A fire burned in a nearby fireplace, providing welcome warmth against the chill of the spring afternoon.

A man who had been seated at a leather recliner near the fireplace rose as they entered.

"Gabby? Mija? Qué pasa?" he asked.

"Papi. Mami. You should sit down for this."

IN HER ROLE as a CBI agent, Gabriella had visited families more than once with bad news.

But nothing could have prepared her for this, she thought as she sat across from her parents who sat beside each other on the sofa. Diego took a seat in an adjacent chair.

She wrung her hands together, seeking calm she wasn't feeling. She forced herself to face them as she said, "This is my civilian partner, Diego Rodriguez, and his K-9, Poppy. They're helping me on the case of the missing hiker."

"The young teacher, right? But what does that have to do with us?" her mother asked, gaze darting between her and Diego.

With a sharp dip of her head, she said, "I'm assisting on the investigation, and I believed it was connected to some cold cases I'd been reviewing."

"Cold cases? Like Isabella's?" her father asked, immediately realizing where she was going.

"Yes, like Isabella's. I know we've all been hoping—"

"Of course, we've all been hoping, mija," her mother said in an anguished cry.

Her father laid a hand on her mother's arm to quiet her. "Mi amor. Let Gabby finish. Por favor."

It was like ripping off a bandage, she thought. The faster she did it, the less it would hurt.

"My investigations led me to believe that Isabella was the first victim of a serial killer."

Her mother shouted "no," but Gabriella pushed on. "Today that killer left me Isabella's crucifix."

"No, no, no," her mother wailed, and covered her face with her hands.

"I'm sorry, Mami. Papi. I'd hoped for so long it was just a kidnapping—"

"Just a kidnapping, mija," her father challenged as he wrapped his wife into his arms to offer comfort.

"Yes, Papi. Just a kidnapping, because at least then she'd still be alive," Gabriella said, and jumped to her feet. "We have to go. Whoever did this to Isabella has another woman, and we have to find her. Stop him."

Her father's face was set in stone, all hard edges that deepened the lines of worry and sadness that had been etched onto his features by Isabella's disappearance.

"Go, mija. Do your job. Your mami and I will be here when you can talk more," he said with a slow, respectful dip of his head.

"Thank you, Papi. I'll be back as soon as I can," she said, and hurried to the door.

"I'm very sorry for your loss," Diego said, and chased after her as she dashed outside and almost ran back to Ryder's SUV.

He opened the back door, harnessed Poppy and then popped into the passenger seat. "Are you okay?"

With a heavy sigh, she said, "As well as can be expected. We need to find this guy. We can't let him kill another woman."

"He won't. We'll stop him. Let's get back to CPS and see what additional info they've found so far."

"Agreed," she said, and pulled away from the curb.

HE SLIPPED INTO the bushes of the house across the street from the Ruiz home.

He'd gone straight there after leaving the office, certain that Gabriella—what a beautiful name for a beautiful woman—would head straight to her parents' home once they left the scout camp.

He hadn't been wrong, but then again, he rarely was.

It was why he was always steps ahead of the police.

Like now, he thought as the black SUV drove away and he slipped onto the sidewalk to watch it drive away. They'd be headed back to the CPS offices, but he was going to linger here for a little bit and enjoy the show inside the family home.

Her parents were visible through the front windows, huddling close together. The pain was visible on their faces as they relived their daughter's death all over again.

Delicious, he thought, feeding on their grief. But not for too long, he reminded himself and buried his head deeper beneath the hoodie he'd slipped on after he'd left the office.

Pivoting on one well-soled heel, he hurried up the block to where he'd parked the Range Rover. The tires and sides of the car were dirty from his earlier trip to the scout camp. He should have cleaned the car before returning to the office, but he hadn't had time, thinking that he had that two o'clock appointment.

He couldn't leave the car dirty, with all that potential evidence on it.

A quick trip to the car wash and then home. To her.

He'd been ignoring Roberts the past day, too seduced by the deliciousness of the older Ruiz sister.

But he couldn't keep her for much longer. So tonight, he'd play with her some more. Maybe tomorrow, too, but after that…

It would be time to get rid of his little toy and think about taking another.

Gabriella came to mind then.

How enticing it was to think about making two sisters his.

Yes, he would have to think about watching her. Wait for the right time.

And when he struck, she wouldn't know what had hit her.

Chapter Fifteen

Jeannie heard footsteps above and carefully eased the two bolts back into the wall. With a sweep of the flimsy blanket he had given her, she tried her best to hide the dust from the plaster she had worked away from the bolts.

It was hard to tell how successful she'd been in the nonexistent light in the cellar.

As he snapped on the stage lights, they stunned her again with their intensity, and she worried they'd display the remnants of her handiwork.

He stepped down the rest of the stairs and stood before her, camera in hand.

She took a quick look at the floor and fear filled her as she saw the telltale white of the wall dust.

"That's it. I love seeing that fear," he said, not realizing the reason for the fear.

She used that opportunity to push the blanket off and over the dust, and tilted her chin defiantly, knowing he liked that too.

"I'm not afraid of you. You're nothing but a loser who has to tie up women to have them," she said, and raised her hands to prove her point, careful not to dislodge the bolt she had worked free.

"Feisty today, aren't you?" he said with a laugh, raised the camera and snapped off some photos.

She cursed him, but he only laughed and set aside the camera.

"I'll miss you, Jeannie. You've been one of the better ones," he said as he approached.

Time was running out, she realized. She sensed it in his mood. But she wasn't going to go out without a fight. She'd make sure that she was going to be the last woman he took.

MUCH LIKE GABRIELLA, Diego hated that the killer was always two steps ahead of them.

The tracker.

Following them to the scout camp.

And now this.

"Yes, Papi. I understand. Thanks for letting us know," she said as she disconnected the call she had just put on speaker.

"How did he know where your parents live?" Diego asked as Gabriella settled into the seat beside him.

With a shake of her head, she said, "It wouldn't be hard. They've lived there forever, and when Isabella disappeared, the house was all over the news."

"We can go back and look for cameras along the street. See what they've recorded," Diego said, and peered around the table at everyone gathered there.

"Definitely, but first, let's go over what we've got so far," Sophie said, and with a quick look at Ryder, urged him to proceed.

"CSI techs say they found DNA on Isabella's crucifix. They're processing it right now, and we should have something in a few hours," he advised.

"They'll run it through CODIS. But what if Konijn isn't already in there?" Gabriella said, and nervously tapped the table with her hand.

"Then we'll check it against any genealogy sites we can access. If we're lucky—" Robbie began, but Gabriella cut him off.

"We haven't been lucky so far."

Diego laid a hand on hers to quiet the nervous motion. "I haven't known you long, but I know you probably have more than luck going on, right, Robbie?" he said to take down the temperature in the room.

"We got the VIN for Hughes's wife's Range Rover, but we didn't have to go to the vehicle manufacturer for location info. She works at the hospital, and CCTV puts the car at the hospital the morning you were followed."

"Do we take him off the list then?" Diego asked.

"Not off, but he's lower with the info we gathered," Ryder said, and prompted Sophie for her report.

"We were able to get the carrier from the SIM card on the tracker. Which is back on Gabriella's car—but more on that later," Sophie said.

"I got a warrant, and the carrier provided the name of the account holder. It's an LLC that looks to be a shell company," Ryder advised.

"We checked the Secretary of State records and got a name and street address for the Registered Agent. It turns out he's an attorney who represents Konijn's wealth management firm," Robbie said, pulled some papers from a file, and passed them across the table to Diego and Gabriella.

Diego took a look at the business record and then held up the papers as he asked, "Is this enough to bring in father and son?"

"No. Not yet, but soon," Gabriella said with a tired sigh.

Diego was sure there was more the two tech geniuses had found. "Any luck on the partial plates or the CCTV feeds?"

"We were able to get a better read on the plate from one of the CCTV feeds, and we gave that info to Ryder," Robbie said, and glanced at the CBI agent.

"Plate came back to a gray Range Rover registered to a different shell company," Ryder said.

"Let me guess. Same Registered Agent?" Gabriella said, and Ryder nodded.

"Just how many shell companies do the Konijns have?" Diego wondered aloud.

"Glad you asked," Sophie said and pulled out a sheath of papers she handed over. "Sorry, it's only one copy, but I didn't want to kill more trees."

The report was nearly an inch thick. Together they skimmed through all the pages of business records as Sophie said, "These are all companies the lawyer acting as the Registered Agent has set up, which may include people other than the Konijns."

"How do we limit it to just them?" Diego said.

"You don't need much to register a company. Fill out a simple form and pay, that's it," Sophie said, but Robbie immediately jumped in with more.

"We assumed that their offices and homes might be held in the names of one or more of the LLCs. Bingo, we connected the office and homes to three of these shell companies."

"I think that with this info we have enough to at least bring in the Konijns for additional questioning," Ryder said.

"I want to be there when you do the interviews," Gabriella said, fresh determination in her voice.

"I'll call and set it up for first thing in the morning," he said.

"You know they're going to lawyer up, right?" she pressed.

"Of course, but they'll be rattled," Ryder said with a smile.

Gabriella likewise smiled and said, "And when they're rattled, they may make a mistake."

"I guess that in the meantime, Gabriella and I will go back to Highlands Square and check for cameras that might have gotten video of our killer," Diego said with a glance at her.

"We will, but you mentioned not removing the tracker. Why?" she asked the team at the table.

"Don't want to tip him off until we exhaust all possibilities at the carrier. We've also put another tracker on the car so that we can follow you as well in case he removes his. The most important thing is to keep you safe. We all think his leaving you Isabella's crucifix is an escalation that says you're next," Ryder said.

Gabriella nodded. "I agree. Maybe that's another way to draw him out. Using me as bait."

Diego slashed his hands through the air. "No way. That's too dangerous."

Gabriella took hold of one of his hands and said, "If we have to do it to get Jeannie Roberts back, I'm willing to take that risk."

Diego inhaled deeply, held it and then released it with a rush of words. "I'm going to be on you like white on rice," he said.

Gabriella wanted to assert, as she had before, that she could take care of herself.

But in the short time they'd gotten to know each other, she knew he respected her and what she could do.

Because of that, she didn't challenge him over his protectiveness.

Instead, she pushed ahead with an idea that Diego had proposed earlier that day while they were at the scout camp.

"While Diego and I go back to my parents', do you think you could check on something?"

"Of course. What is it?" Sophie said as she gathered the papers they had reviewed during the meeting.

Gabriella did a quick look at Diego. "While we were at the scout camp, Diego raised the possibility that the killer may have brought back Isabella to the area after the searches were completed."

Ryder dipped his head from side to side as he considered it. "Possible but risky."

"It was his first. He probably wasn't as…regimented," Diego pointed out, and immediately fixed his attention on Sophie and Ryder. "You've used lidar in the past to find ground anomalies, right?"

"We have. On multiple occasions," Robbie confirmed with a dip of his head.

"Do you think you can do it in the area around the scout camp?" Gabriella asked.

"Possibly. We'll reach out to our contacts in the area," Sophie confirmed.

"Great. Do you think you could do one other thing?" Diego asked with another glance at the report from the company register.

"Sure. What is it?" Sophie asked, gaze intense as she looked at the thick pile of paper.

"Can you see what other properties those LLCs own? See if any are in the general area of either the scout camp or the trails where those women were taken?"

"We can work on that. We can also have Wilson see what other info he can get for those shell companies," Robbie replied, and slapped his hands on the table. "I don't know about you all, but I need a break and—"

"Food. You always need food," Sophie said with a laugh and shake of her head.

"Yes, I do. And it'll give us a break to think over everything we've discussed and make sure we didn't miss anything," he said, rose and walked over to the credenza where he picked up one of the many menus sitting there.

"Chinese, anyone?" he asked.

AS SHE DROVE her car toward her parents', she recalled a joke that a comedian had told about Chinese food and how it seemed they could make it even faster than you could order it.

The food had come quickly, but they'd still managed to walk Poppy so she could relieve herself and fed her while Sophie and Robbie had laid out the dishes they'd ordered.

Hunger and the need to move the investigation along had made for a quick dinner.

"Do you think we'll find anything?" Gabriella asked, and looked at him as they returned to Highlands Square. The lights from the passing streetlamps cast patterns on his handsome face as they drove.

"We will. Too many people have those doorbells now, capturing everything that goes on," he said, and it was impossible to miss his tone.

"Too many? I guess you're not a fan?"

With a shrug, he said, "People complain about invasions of privacy all the time and yet they put out so much info willingly. Social media. Doorbell cameras. Cell phones. Virtual assistants that turn on our lights or answer our questions. They all create breaks in our privacy."

She understood that more than most. They regularly used that kind of info and more, like toll payment devices, to track and catch criminals.

"It's not always a bad thing," she said, earning a rough laugh from him.

"No, it isn't. It makes our lives easier at times. But I wonder if people know just how much they're giving up."

"Probably not," she said as she pulled up in front of her parents' home. Before she left the car, she looked around. "My father thought he spotted someone watching from across the street. Near those bushes," she said, and pointed in the direction of the home opposite her parents.

"Let's see if Poppy can pick up a scent," he said, and slipped from the passenger seat.

She left the car and then waited for Diego to swing around with Poppy. Together they crossed the street, and he commanded Poppy to search.

"*Such*," he said.

Poppy nosed around the bushes and then took off along the sidewalk, head down as she seemingly followed a scent.

The home with the bushes didn't have a doorbell camera, but the next one did. If the killer had passed this way, he would have been seen.

But they didn't stop to check. They let Poppy continue along, searching, until she stopped in front of one home, went to the curb, and then nosed around some more before lying down.

"The scent stopped here. This is where he must have had his car," Diego said, and glanced back in the direction in which they had come. Motioning with his hand, he said, "At least two doorbell cameras on this side."

Turning, he scrutinized the homes on the opposite side of the street. "One more there," he said, and pointed in the direction of a home.

"Great. Let's start on this side and see if the owners have video and if so, if they're willing to share it," she said.

Diego nodded, and they backtracked to the first house with a doorbell camera.

A young father with a toddler on his hip answered. His gaze narrowed in puzzlement as Gabriella held up her badge.

"How can I help you?" he asked, and then called for his wife to come and take the toddler.

She hurried over and took the boy away, but not before shooting her husband a worried look.

"There's nothing to worry about, Mr.—"

"Evans. Chris Evans like the actor," he said with a smile.

"CBI Agent Ruiz and this is my civilian consultant, Agent Rodriguez. We see that you have a doorbell camera, and we're wondering if you might have recorded something earlier this afternoon. Around four o'clock?"

He shrugged. "It's possible. People on the sidewalk trip the motion detector. Honestly, it's frustrating at times," he said and wiped a hand across his short-cropped hair, which rasped with the motion.

Gabriella handed him her business card. "If you wouldn't mind checking, we would appreciate you sending it to my email."

"Sure, no problem," he said, whipped out his phone and

swiped the screen. With a nod, he said, "I do have it. Some guy in a hoodie walking by. I'll send it."

"Great, and thank you," she said.

"Anything we should worry about?" the young father said.

Gabriella and Diego shared a look. "Make sure to keep your doors locked, and if you have an alarm system, set it. Just as a precaution. We're working on the case involving the missing hiker."

He nodded. "Thanks for that advice. I'll let my wife know as well," he said, and closed the door.

They repeated that visit at the two other homes they had identified earlier and luckily, each of the homes had video of the hooded man and promised to send it. The one home had even captured him climbing into a gray Range Rover, confirming that it had likely been the killer watching Gabriella and her parents.

When they returned to their car, Diego said, "You should send those videos to Sophie and Robbie. They may be able to clean them up."

She nodded, whipped out her phone and did as he'd suggested. "Done. Should we go back to CPS?"

Diego shook his head. "Not yet. My place is on the way back. I'd like to stop there and pick up some things."

"Why?" she asked.

"Because you're not going anywhere without me, and that includes tonight."

Chapter Sixteen

Diego didn't know what she would make of the furnished studio apartment he'd rented until he could find something more permanent once he was sure Crooked Pass Security was the place he was meant to be.

For weeks he'd thought he'd found that place with Jackson in Regina, but fate clearly had another plan for him.

Which made him wonder if it included Gabriella, he thought as she stood by his door, waiting for him to grab some clothes and his toilet kit.

"It's not much, but I wanted to save money while I found the right place," he explained as he set his duffel by the door and then went in search of another bag to pack up what he might need for Poppy.

"It's nice," she said, but he didn't buy it.

"It'll do. I want to volunteer at a local church that hosts a group for veterans with PTSD and also be closer to CPS once I know…once it's more settled," he said.

He hadn't said it outright, but Gabriella had picked up on his uncertainty.

"It's not easy to know where you belong."

He stopped riffling through a cabinet that held Poppy's food and treats. Meeting her gaze from across the room, he said, "It's not."

Grabbing a smaller bag of food and another of treats, he tossed them into a reusable shopping bag.

She was waiting for him by the door still, her gaze fixed on him as he walked over to grab his duffel and did a hand command for Poppy to heel. Poppy immediately came to his side, and he said, "I'm ready when you are."

Gabriella wasn't sure she would ever be ready for this intriguing and complex man.

And although her home wasn't as small as his studio, she wasn't sure it was big enough. She wasn't sure what could be big enough to help her avoid the maelstrom of emotions she felt around him.

But she lied and said, "I'm ready."

With a slight shift of his head, he invited her to open the door, and she did. But then he stopped her and said, "Let me check it out first."

Given that the killer could now be tracking them, she deferred to his request.

He pushed through the door, bags in hand and Poppy at his side.

His studio apartment was ground floor and not far from a private parking lot. Quiet since it was well past dinner hour, and most people were probably getting ready to settle in for the night.

No one was on the grounds or in the parking area. No sign of motion anywhere except for Diego ahead of her with Poppy at his side.

He reached the car and turned, waiting for her.

Like white on rice, she remembered, and realized he meant it.

She hit the fob to unlock all the doors, and when she got to the driver's side, she said, "I appreciate the concern, Diego. I do, but—"

"You can take care of yourself," he said with a crooked grin, dropped one bag and reached up to cup her cheek. "Sometimes it's okay to lean on others."

As she had done the day before, she laid her hand against his chest, directly over his heart, and said, "I'm here if you want to lean sometime, too."

His grin broadened into a wide smile, and he nodded. "I'll remember that."

He opened the door for her. She slipped in, waiting for him to drop his bags onto the floor, harness Poppy and settle into the seat beside her.

Diego's apartment was a short ten-minute ride to the Crooked Pass Security offices, so she understood why he had chosen it. If this investigation was indicative of their workload, he might regularly put in late nights at work. A short commute would make his life easier.

She pulled into the parking lot and a CPS spot that was empty. In no time, she, Diego and Poppy were headed to the elevator bank.

But as they neared, the loud screech of tires snared their attention.

Before she could react, Diego had wrapped her in his arms and dragged her behind the protection of a parked car as a barrage of gunfire peppered the wall behind them and smashed into the parked car. Bits of concrete and shattered glass rained down.

Another loud screech sounded, and then there was nothing but silence.

"Are you okay?" Diego asked as they crouched by the car.

She faced him. His hair was littered with small pieces of concrete and glass. Brushing them away, she said, "I'm fine. You? Poppy?"

He rubbed Poppy's fur, brushing away the debris from the shooting, and then said, "We're okay."

With that, he helped her to her feet. They were about to look for any evidence when a loud pounding from the stairwell stopped them.

Ryder, Robbie and Sophie surged out of the stairwell, faces etched with fear and worry.

"Are you okay?" Ryder asked, and skipped his gaze over all of them.

"We are. Someone's car, not so much," Gabriella said and gestured to the vehicle that had taken the brunt of the damage during the drive-by. Shattered rear windows and pockmarked metal memorialized the violence.

"I'll call CSI and get them working on this, but did you see the car? Shooter?" Ryder asked.

She shook her head and peered at Diego, who had been the one to react before she had realized there was any danger.

"Not a gray Range Rover. Black pickup, I think. Tinted windows. I saw a muzzle. Dark face, maybe a mask," he said, and circled a hand around his face in explanation.

"Let's get upstairs and see what video we can grab from the parking lot cameras," Sophie said, and laid a gentle and comforting hand against her shoulder.

She nodded, and they walked to the elevator bank. As she saw the dings caused by the bullets in the elevator door, it finally sank in.

Someone had tried to kill them.

Her gut chilled and a rough shudder racked her body, but she controlled it. She couldn't let the killer distract her from her primary goal: saving Jeannie Roberts.

If it had been the killer, she thought, baffled by a very different way of attack.

In the CPS conference room, Sophie and Robbie immediately got to work, pulling up video from the parking lot CCTVs.

As they ran the video, it confirmed Diego's initial impressions.

A large black pickup, a Ford F-150, raced from the bowels of the parking lot and screeched to a halt. The tinted window drifted down to reveal the muzzle but not much else.

Muzzle flashes repeated over and over as bullets flew.

A brief silence followed by another screech as the pickup roared out of the parking lot.

Robbie tapped on the keys and rewound the video to the spot where the pickup first appeared. The plates had been obscured, but with another few taps, Robbie was able to reveal the faint outlines of the plate numbers beneath the license plate screen.

"I'll send this to Ryder so he can have DMV give us the owner info," Sophie said as her fingers flew over across her phone screen.

"Chances are it's another fake LLC connected to the Konijns," Diego said, and tossed his pen on the tabletop in frustration.

"Maybe, but I'm not so sure," Gabriella said, and laid a hand over his to offer support.

Puzzled, Diego looked at her as he cupped her hand in his. "Why do you say that?"

"I know serial killers can change how they operate, but this kind of attack won't give them satisfaction. It's not personal enough," she said.

"He can't get his jollies from the pain he inflicts," Robbie said, ever the one to hit the nail on the head.

"That's right," Gabriella said and plowed on. "He wouldn't get any pleasure from something like a drive-by."

"What about the DC sniper attacks?" Sophie asked.

"I see you've been doing some homework," Gabriella said with a nod to the other woman's insightfulness. "When you think about it, they were able to see what that shot did through the scope. See the kill. It wasn't some wild shoot-'em-up like what just happened."

"Makes sense," Diego said, and squeezed her hand before releasing it.

"That leaves us with the evidence we have so far and also, anything you've come up with since we sent over that doorbell camera footage," Gabriella said, and glanced across the table to the two tech geniuses.

Robbie nodded and quickly pulled up some images onto the monitor on the wall. "We were able to snag these images of our unsub from that footage. Similar height, weight and build to the suspect from the other night. Big difference: the pants," he said and zoomed in on that element in two different sets of photos. "The other night he was wearing jeans. Tonight, they look like dress pants. The kind you might wear at a fancy office."

"Like Konijn's wealth management firm," Diego said.

"Like that. Given the timing, he may have left the office and not had time to change. He just tossed the hoodie and jacket over what he was wearing," Sophie replied.

Diego and Gabriella shared a look before she said, "And this height, weight and build are similar to the younger Konijn, right?"

Sophie nodded and displayed a copy of Peter Konijn's driver's license. "He matches the height and weight we guesstimated from the videos. You've seen him in person, so you'd be a better judge as to the build."

"Definitely in the range," Diego confirmed.

Satisfied with that, Gabriella pushed on with what they had discussed earlier that day. "Any luck on the properties owned by the LLCs or the possible lidar imaging?"

"Too much luck," Sophie said with a tired sigh, and a second later, a map with at least three dozen red dots filled the monitor. "These are all the properties we suspect are owned by possible Konijn LLCs."

"We eliminated any locations that were multiuser dwellings. Figured it would be too much of a risk for him to transport women," Robbie said, and with a few taps of his keyboard, about two dozen of the marked locations dropped off the map.

"That's a logical assumption, but it still leaves almost a dozen places," Gabriella said as she scrutinized the map.

"It does. So we asked Wilson to overlay these sites with the locations for our victims and provide a probability as to where the killer might be," Sophie said as her fingers flew across her keyboard. When she was finished, six places were now shown with bright green dots and a number.

"Does that number reflect the probability of it being the killer's location?" Diego said, beating her to the question.

"Yes. So for this location, the probability is 75 percent that it's where our unsub and hopefully Roberts will be," Sophie said, and used a laser pointer to highlight that spot on the map.

"And that's based on what?" Gabriella pressed, trying to understand how Wilson and his program could pinpoint the locations.

Sophie nodded and with a grim smile, passed a report across the table. "This report shows the variables considered to reach this conclusion. Things like proximity to the attacks and disappearances. Also, the nature of the house. For example, ranch or colonial—"

"Because who wants to lug a body up and down stairs," Diego said as he flipped through the pages of the report.

"Possible but harder to do. But also, did they own it at the time of each attack or kidnap," Robbie explained.

So many variables that would have taken them many workhours, if not days, to gather and Wilson's program had done it in only a few hours.

"Pretty amazing but also pretty scary," he said.

"AI and programs like this can be intimidating, but they won't ever replace human intuition," Sophie said.

Diego nodded and closed the report. "Do you mind if I take this for a deeper look?"

"Not at all. You might spot something the program didn't. It's not foolproof," Sophie said and motioned for him to keep it.

Maybe not foolproof, but he could see how it could make

an investigator feel foolish at not making the connections as quickly as the program, he thought.

Gabriella moved on with, "What about the lidar imaging?"

Robbie's lips thinned into a knife-sharp slash, and he shook his head. "There are only a couple of people in our area who can help us with that and unfortunately, they are all out of town to work on a gig investigating Mayan ruins."

"We reached out to others, but they can't make it for a few days. By then it might be too late," Sophie said, but as she had done before, she worked the keys and brought up another map.

"We do have this," she said.

"Let me guess. Wilson's program," Diego said as he scrutinized the map. Rising, he walked to the monitor and pointed to one area on the map. "This is the scout camp, right?"

Sophie nodded. "It is. Just like Wilson used certain parameters to select those properties, he did the same here. Things like where the attacks and disappearances occurred and also, height and weight of the individuals and how far someone might be able to carry them."

As Diego watched, a transparent purple circle appeared in an area just above the location of the scout camp. "This is the possible killing field?" he asked.

Robbie nodded. "That's the area where he's likely to have brought his victims. We relied on your theory that since this was the site of his first kill, it would be special to him."

He turned to examine Gabriella, who was studying the map intently. "You're familiar with the area. Does that seem plausible?"

She did a little sway of her head and then nodded. "Like I mentioned earlier, the trails only go partly up the mountain and the area Wilson's identified is past that. But it doesn't preclude that it's possible."

Ryder came to the door of the conference room, his face set in hard lines. He held up his smartphone and said, "We've got a hit on the license plate number on that Ford F-150."

Chapter Seventeen

"Great. Is it to one of the LLCs or Konijn?" Gabriella asked.

Ryder shook his head and walked over to the table. "It's not. I just sent you the info, Sophie. Can you pull it up?"

She did, replacing the map image with copies of a driver's license and a rap sheet.

"Jack Hayes. Petty criminal. Arrested several times for drug dealing and assault and burglary. Currently free because of our new no-bail policies," Ryder said with an angry sigh. "I've put a BOLO out for him."

"Seems like someone hired to intimidate us?" Diego said.

Ryder did a sharp bob of his head. "Definitely. That drive-by was a warning. We're getting close."

That wasn't sitting right with Gabriella. She slashed her hand through the air and said, "Our killer has been extremely careful until now. Why would he hire someone like Hayes to take potshots at us?"

"People have done stupider things," Diego offered in explanation.

She wasn't buying it. "This just seems like a diversion to pull us away from what's important."

"I can't disagree. Hopefully, an officer will spot him and bring him in. In the meantime, what have you been up to while I was gone?" Ryder asked.

They quickly filled him in on the prospective locations identified and for review, Sophie pulled up the two maps side by side.

Ryder surveyed them and said, "Six is still a lot of places to visit."

"I agree. I think we should visit the Konijns and see how they react to questions about the LLCs and these particular properties," Gabriella said.

"Agreed. We can do that first thing in the morning," Ryder said, then glanced at Sophie. "Can you print out a list of those six properties—maybe even a photo?"

"I can have that for you first thing in the a.m.," she confirmed.

Gabriella peered at Diego and said, "If the weather's good tomorrow, do you think we could take Poppy into that area identified by Wilson and search for…" She couldn't finish as the possibility of finally finding her sister nearly overwhelmed her.

Diego skimmed the back of his hand across her cheek and said, "We can go find Isabella."

"Great," she said with a strangled sigh, and then glanced at the others. "Unless we get something overnight, I guess I'll see you at the Konijns' at 9:00 a.m."

"I'll be there," Ryder confirmed with a dip of his head.

"Sophie and I will keep working on some leads. Maybe see if there are any connections between Hayes and the Konijns," Robbie said.

"Thank you. Diego and I will be at my place if you need us," she said and slowly rose, exhaustion pulling at her after the long and emotional day.

"Get some rest," Ryder called out as they walked out of the room.

She felt guilty because she suspected that her colleagues would be at work long after Diego and she had gone home.

Diego. Home, she thought, and spared a glance at the man standing beside her with Poppy at his side.

She couldn't remember the last time a man other than her father had been in her home, mostly because she wasn't the kind for one-night stands or long relationships for that matter. She'd been too consumed by work and by her search for the truth behind her sister's disappearance.

Having him there again, in her space, was going to be a challenge on multiple levels. But if the killer had turned his attention to her with his little gift, it made sense to have added protection.

He must have sensed her turmoil, because he slipped an arm around her waist and drew her into a comforting embrace.

"I know it's been rough for you today," he whispered, and hugged her.

"That's an understatement," she said with a rough laugh.

"Some rest may help," he said as the elevator arrived and they stepped onboard.

Silence reigned on the way down to the parking lot.

He stepped in front of her as the doors opened, providing protection, but the CSI team was still there and finishing up.

It was safe for now, she thought as he gently touched the small of her back and they hurried to her car. In steps that were becoming familiar, he loaded Poppy into the back, harnessed her and then joined her in the front seat.

He faced her then and skimmed the back of his hand down her cheek. "Let's get home and get some rest. Tomorrow may be a rough day."

She nodded and tried to force tomorrow from her mind, especially if Diego's theory was supported by Wilson's program, finally leading them to Isabella.

"If I remember correctly, your home isn't far?" he said as she pulled out of the parking lot.

She chuckled and was about to reply when he beat her to it.

"Twenty minutes, right," he said with a laugh.

"About that," she confirmed with a slight smile as she made the few turns to access the highway.

She was grateful that Diego remained silent during the ride. She was too busy processing all that had happened that day and what it meant not only about her sister but more importantly how to save Jeannie Roberts.

Her gut told her Jeannie was still alive.

No program or AI could ever do that, she thought, recalling all the info that Wilson had provided in just a few short hours.

As she pulled up in front of her modest Craftsman-style home, it occurred to her that she'd been on autopilot as she drove. But as it did every time she got there, a sense of peace enveloped her.

Until she realized that the handsome and complex man sitting beside her would again be passing through the doors into what she considered her fortress of solitude.

"We're home," she said with a forced smile.

"Good. Let's get you settled inside and then I'll take Poppy for a walk around the grounds to make sure it's all secure," he said, and once again skimmed the back of his hand across her cheek, offering comfort.

"Okay."

DIEGO HAD HER back as they walked to the front door of the beautiful but simple home. As it had the first time, it brought a feeling of comfort.

An open gable marked the edges of a large front porch. At one end was a wooden bench with some pillows and on the other, two comfortable-looking Adirondack chairs bracketing a small table with a metal lantern.

He could picture her sitting there, in this quiet neighborhood, watching the world go by and in more ways than one.

Much like he had lost a portion of his life to the PTSD that had chased him after his service, she had let her determination to find her sister steal part of her life.

The pillars holding up the porch and part of the siding were done in a white-and-gray stone that matched the dark charcoal color of the board-and-batten siding. All those neutral colors made the natural color of large double wooden doors pop, even at night.

Two modern black-and-white sconces cast a welcoming glow, and she unlocked the door and they stepped into an open living room/dining/kitchen area. Directly above the kitchen was a loft to her office area.

"You can use the guest bedroom again," she said with a wave of her hand toward the room.

"If you don't mind, I'd like to make sure the area is clear," he said, and at her nod, he walked Poppy through her home.

In front and to the right there was a utility room and what could have been a third bedroom, only she was using it as a home gym.

A bathroom separated that bedroom from the one in the back she wanted him to use, although he'd likely take the couch this time because it gave him a better vantage point on most of the entrances into her home.

On the left-hand side in the back was her bedroom and he entered that area mindfully, moving to the French doors by her bed to make sure they were locked. The doors faced a fenced-in yard. Moonlight silvered the green of the grass and the bushes and spring bulbs blooming along the edges.

He pushed past the bed to a spacious bathroom, again in neutral colors and stone.

Behind the bathroom was a nice-sized walk-in closet.

All clear, he thought, and as he walked back out, it hit him.

Her rooms smelled like her, fresh and flowery, and his body responded to her scent.

He sucked in a breath to quell the desire. What a mistake. Her scent only wrapped around him deeper, making him ache.

"Everything okay?" she asked as he returned to the main living area, mistaking the reason for his worry.

"We're good here. I'm going to take Poppy for a walk around

the grounds and then feed her if that's okay," he said, and Poppy sat beside him, waiting for another command.

"Mi casa es su casa," she said, hands wide in invitation.

It would be easy to see this as a home with her. The space was welcoming. Homey.

But as quickly as he thought that, guilt nearly swamped him as he remembered his fallen brothers who would never see home again.

Forcing a smile, he said, "Gracias. I won't be long."

He dashed out the front door and walked with Poppy all around the front of the home, seeing if she would pick up any scents the way she had on the sidewalk earlier.

Nothing on the front porch.

The house didn't have a garage, so he led Poppy around the side and to the gate for the white vinyl fence that encircled the yard.

Inside the backyard, he walked Poppy all around and to the far end, but again she didn't pick up on anything. He unleashed her and let her run free for a few minutes while he again checked the French doors to Gabriella's bedroom. They were locked, and she had drawn the curtains to close off the space.

His bedroom also had French doors, and he checked them. Locked as well.

Satisfied, he watched as Poppy relieved herself. Quickly he cleaned up, leashed her and walked back to the front of the house. Entering, he found Gabriella sitting at the kitchen table with the report that Sophie had handed him and a large black mug.

"I made some coffee," she said. Not that she needed to tell him—the earthy and comfy scent of it spiced the air.

"Thanks. I could use something warm," he said, and rubbed his hands together before freeing Poppy of her leash and harness.

With a hand command, he led her to the kitchen where he

filled collapsible bowls with water and kibble and set them off to one side on the floor.

Gabriella had left him a mug on the counter, and he prepped his coffee, joined her at the table and sat kitty-corner to her.

Poppy gobbled down her kibble and meandered over to sit at their feet.

"There's a lot of info in that report," he said, and flipped a hand in the direction of the inch-thick pile of paper in front of Gabriella.

She had opened to the first page and tapped it. "Like Sophie said, these are the six locations with the highest probability based on a lot of variables."

"You have doubts about the criteria he used?" Diego said, and leaned in to watch her expressive face. The doubt was apparent as she picked up her mug, leaned back and scrutinized the page.

"Certain kinds of homes scored lower for various reasons, including apartment buildings. But several serial killers did their work in apartment buildings. Jeffrey Dahmer, for example," she said.

"So you would add more locations to investigate?" he asked, worried that with the clock ticking, such a task would be impossible.

With a hesitant shake of her head, she said, "That would add too many, because the Konijns have tons of rental properties. And yes, it makes sense to flag single-family homes first. Many serial killers used their properties to bury their victims."

"Should we look for remains there first instead of the scout camp?" he asked, although his gut told him that the killer might have a stronger connection to that site.

Shrugging, she said, "I agree with you that if Isabella was his first victim, that might make the scout camp special."

She jabbed a finger between two locations identified by Wilson's program. "These are ranked as lower probability. We'd have to dig through all this to find out why," she said, and riffled through the pages of the report. "But I think these should be higher on our list. They're closer to the scout camp, for starters. Single-family with larger properties. No neighbors to hear or see what's happening."

"We can start with those after we interview the Konijns," he said and bent to rub Poppy's head.

"I'm calling it a night," she said, although he suspected that she'd be thinking about the case as she lay in bed, much like he'd be running through all the info that had been dumped on them.

He rose as well, a little slower as she stood there, waiting for him. For what he wondered until she leaned toward him, cupped his cheek and dropped a kiss on his lips.

"Thank you for all that you're doing," she whispered against his lips.

Her lips were warm and oh so sweet and when she didn't immediately pull away, he cradled the back of her skull with his hand and said, "I want to help you find peace, Gabriella."

She kissed him again, a slow, leisurely kiss that held the promise of more until she reluctantly took a step back. "We should get some rest. I'll set the house alarm from my room."

Before he could say a word, she hurried away and closed the door.

A little whine from Poppy had him looking at his dog, who was peering at him with a look that seemed to say, "Are you just going to let her go?"

"Yes, Poppy, I am. It's not the right time," he said, and with a wave of his hand, he commanded Poppy to follow him to the guest bedroom.

As he entered, he heard a loud beep warning that she'd set the alarm. Because of that, he didn't open the French doors to check the backyard once again. But with the bright moonlight, he could see that all was quiet there.

He undressed and showered, feeling as if he had to wash off all that had happened that day, from the tumble at the scout camp to the drive-by that had his back aching from protecting Gabriella.

Gabriella, he thought as he ran soapy hands across the assorted bruises and scars on his body.

Stellar-shaped scars from when he'd been shot on deployment. The harder, pronounced ridges along his ribs and lower from the shrapnel created by the rocket that had brought down his helicopter and killed so many of his brothers.

He was damaged goods, and his wounds were the least of it. Not the kind of man for someone like Gabriella.

He finished the shower, toweled off, slipped on sweatpants and climbed into bed, wincing as his back once again protested the movement.

Resting his head on his hands, he inhaled deeply. The pillows and sheets smelled like her. He closed his eyes, picturing her. Imagined what it would be like to have a wife and kids. He hadn't thought about that in years. He'd been too busy rebuilding himself. Trying to put the pieces of who he had been back together and helping others do the same.

But as he drifted off to sleep, imagining that new beginning, the darkness came again, clawing at him. Pulling him back into an abyss that he'd thought he'd escaped years earlier.

"No, no, no," he called out, and flailed as bullets ripped into his body and the sound of gunshots echoed in his brain.

The scent of sulfur attacked his senses until another achingly familiar aroma wafted in.

Gabriella, he thought, and suddenly she was there in his arms. Warm, but it was a wet warmth, and he realized she was bleeding.

"No, no, no," he wailed in anguish. *This is just a dream*, he told himself as he tried to get a grip on ground that seemed to disintegrate beneath his fingertips until they dug into something warm and solid and real.

Chapter Eighteen

A noise had dragged Gabriella from a troubled sleep.

She couldn't identify it at first but then realized it was Diego, shouting out.

Grabbing her Glock, she raced from her room into his, expecting a fight.

The fight she found was Diego still asleep, wrestling his demons.

Poppy was at the foot of the bed, whining in sympathy.

As he flailed and called out again, she laid her gun on a nearby dresser and carefully approached him. Kneeling on the bed, she caught his muscled arms as he raised them as if to ward off an attack.

"No, no, no," he cried out, the pain of his dreams all too real.

"Diego, wake up, Diego," she said softly as she ran her hands down his arms to his shoulders to comfort him.

His eyes opened, dark and full of agony, but as he painfully dug his fingers into her upper arms, it was obvious he was still lost in that private hell.

"Diego, por favor. Wake up," she pleaded, and winced at the strength of his grip.

Like a light snapping to life, his eyes suddenly lost their glazed look. As he focused on her and realized he had a death grip on her arms, he loosened his hold and muttered a curse.

"I'm sorry. I'm so sorry," he said, and tenderly ran his hands across the marks on her arms that said she'd have bruises by the morning.

She brushed her fingers through the longer locks of his hair and murmured, "It's okay. You were having a nightmare."

And now that it was over, she realized how compromising her position was, straddling his hips, hands pinning his shoulders to the mattress as she'd struggled to keep him from hurting himself.

"I should go," she said, but he raised his hands, which had drifted to her hips, and cradled her back, drawing her down to rest along the length of his body.

"I don't want to be alone anymore," he said softly and with such anguish, she couldn't leave.

She pulled up the disheveled bedsheets and comforter and snuggled into his chest.

He wrapped his arms around her, kissed her temple and whispered, "Thank you."

Running her hand down his arm, she grasped his hand, and said, "Sometimes it's easier if you share."

His rough laugh vibrated against her core. "I'm not sure it could ever be easy."

"Try," she said, and rose slightly to watch his face as he answered.

TRY. HOW MANY times had he told himself to try to forget as he'd battled to overcome the traumas of war that had followed him into civilian life?

"I told you I struggled with PTSD. It's not the kind of thing that just goes away," he said, and plowed on. "Things can trigger it, like today's gunfire. It was in my dream. You were in my dream," he said, and cradled her cheek.

"You were shot. I felt your blood on my hands just like I felt the blood of my brothers," he said, hand trembling against her soft skin. He stroked his thumb across her cheek and in his mind, it left a smear of blood there.

"I'm okay, Diego. It was just a dream," she said as she realized his nightmare was taking hold again. To draw him back, she cupped his face in both hands and nuzzled his nose with hers.

"It's okay," she crooned, and brushed her lips against his over and over, trying to soothe. Little by little, the stiffness that had been in his body seconds earlier relaxed, and his choppy breaths slowed and lengthened.

He brushed back a lock of her hair that had fallen forward and gently tucked it behind her ear. "Thank you."

"Anything for my partner," she said, offered him a small smile and stroked her thumbs across his cheeks. His skin was smooth there but beneath her palms, there was the rasp of his evening beard.

The edge of his lips tipped up in a precursor to his boyish grin and he slipped his thumb across her smiling lips, his chocolate-colored eyes dark, almost bottomless.

She could lose herself in those eyes, she thought as another emotion slowly crept in.

He skimmed her lips again with his finger and tracked that motion with his gaze. "This could be a big mistake," he said, voice in low tones and husky.

"It could. But there's only one way to find out," she said, and before he could protest, she covered his lips with hers in a kiss that invited him to join her.

She'd dragged him from his hell just moments before and now she was promising him a heaven he hadn't thought possible.

He groaned and opened his mouth to her, accepting that promise. Kissing her over and over until Poppy's whine registered to his ears. She had heard his groan and misinterpreted.

"*Aus*," he said, and with a wave of his hand, instructed her to leave the room.

"It's like having a child," she said with a laugh and then kissed him again.

He joined her in that happiness, chuckling as he wrapped his arms around her, rolled and pressed her into the mattress.

She drifted her hands to his back, holding him close as they kissed until desire roused, and kissing alone wasn't enough.

He rolled again and she straddled him, and waited, her midnight-dark eyes suddenly questioning, as if asking, "Are we sure?"

For the first time in forever, he could say he'd never been more sure of anything in his life.

"WE'RE SURE."

Those two words loosed the last of the bonds keeping them from fulfilling the attraction that had been building between them for days.

She grabbed the hem of her nightshirt, jerked it over her head and tossed it aside.

He skimmed his hands up her sides to cup her breasts, and her body shook with need.

"You're so beautiful," he said as he caressed her.

She mimicked his actions, running her hands down his arms to his broad shoulders, and then down to rest on his chest. She couldn't miss the damage on his warrior's body that marred his physical perfection.

He was all lean, sculpted muscle beneath tanned skin that was smooth except for the scars of war. Scars that weren't limited to his body.

Scars like those she carried in her heart.

For what remained of this night, she wanted peace for both of them and released herself to the pleasure of his touch.

Bending, she kissed him, opening her mouth to his. Inviting him to join her in that peace and satisfaction.

He slipped his hands around to her back and urged her beneath the bedcovers and his naked body. Warmth filled her as skin met skin, and she sighed as that warmth slipped into her.

"You feel amazing," he said as he ran his hands up and down her back, and then guided them to her hips, where her center cradled his hard length.

She moved, and they both moaned as passion rose.

He kissed and caressed her breasts, urging her on until the shift of her hips nearly undid them both.

"Protection," she whispered urgently, seeking completion.

"Wallet. Nightstand," he said, and she leaned over, grabbed it and fumbled to remove a condom.

She hurriedly sheathed him in the protection, and he rolled, trapping her beneath him, but then hesitated, his dark gaze questioning.

She answered that question by rising, kissing his lips and then whispering, "Por favor, Diego."

IT HAD BEEN so long since he'd been with a woman. Maybe never with a woman like Gabriella.

She deserved better than him, but for now, he wanted to be her man.

He found her center and tenderly eased within her. Waited for her to accept his possession, and as she moaned against his lips, pleading for more, he answered that plea.

He moved, driving them both ever higher to the peak of passion. When it came, he groaned with the pleasure of it and stilled inside her to savor her release and his, kissing her deeply. Wanting their union to last forever.

As their climax ebbed, he lowered himself onto her, shifting to one side slightly to keep his weight off.

He stroked back her hair and dropped a kiss on her cheek.

Struggling to find the words to share what he felt, the simple touch of her index finger against his lips spared him that.

"We should get some rest," she said, and then snuggled into his side.

Wrapping his arms around her, he held her close, and her warmth bathed his body.

He savored that warmth and the feel of her, so soft and yielding against him.

It had been too long and never like this. Never with a woman like her, he thought again as the image of her beside him blurred as sleep slowly pulled him away.

When the dreams came this time, he wasn't at war. He was with her, hiking along a bright, sunny mountain trail. She was in front of him, looked over her shoulder at him and smiled.

He smiled back and tugged her hand to haul her close only…

A baby tucked into a carrier. Dark-haired and dark-eyed like the two of them.

Gently he ran a hand over the baby's wisps of brown-black hair, and his heart filled with joy.

"He's beautiful, Gabriella."

She rose on tiptoes and kissed him, lips warm against his.

But something slowly pulled him from the dream to reality.

Her lips, shifting against his.

As he opened his eyes, he realized she was straddling him again and kissing him, a welcoming smile on her face.

"You were grinning in your sleep. I can't resist that grin," she said, and ran a hand through his hair to tame the longer locks.

"You can't?" he said, and grinned for real.

"I can't," she said, and pressed him back against the mattress.

GABRIELLA RAN SOAPY hands across her body and fought the desire that instantly rose after a night and early morning of making love with him.

She rinsed off the soap but couldn't leave the shower just

yet. She needed time alone to process all the info Crooked Pass Security had provided and what was happening with Diego.

Diego, she thought as she finally shut off the warm water and grabbed a towel.

There were lots of things she hadn't expected during this investigation. But the biggest thing she hadn't expected was him.

She didn't regret what had happened. On the contrary.

She would do it again. Oh, how she would happily do it again.

There was the pleasure factor, of course, but it was more than that.

She didn't know how that was possible in only a few short days, but she knew it.

With a self-deprecating laugh, she recalled how her parents had said that they knew from the very first they were meant to be together.

While thinking it romantic, she'd pooh-poohed it to herself, not wanting to rain on her parents' parade.

As she finished drying off, she thought that maybe she'd been too quick to doubt them.

She exited her bathroom and quickly dressed, donning a pale blue blouse and one of the many dark blue pantsuits that screamed cop.

Opening her bedroom door, she was greeted by the enticing smells of bacon and toast, and the sight of Diego cooking at her stove.

He half turned and grinned, and her heart did that little stutter it did whenever he gifted her that boyish grin.

"I hope you don't mind, but I thought we might need to fuel up for today," he said, and dipped his head in the direction of the breakfast bar.

He'd set the table and laid out dishes with bacon slices and a high pile of toast.

As he finished at the stove, she realized he'd made scrambled eggs.

"Thanks," she said, accepted the plate he handed her and followed him to the breakfast bar.

"There's coffee, too," he said, and gestured to the mugs he'd set on the table.

"I'll get us some," she said.

In no time she was back at the breakfast bar and sitting beside him, eating. She hadn't realized how hungry she was until the first fork of creamy scrambled eggs had her almost shoveling them into her mouth.

"You're a good cook," she said as she took a break to sip her coffee and grab a slice of perfectly crispy bacon.

"My mami taught us. She thought all the boys should learn to cook," he said with a smile that reached into his dark eyes.

"She did a good job," she said, and snared a piece of buttered toast. "Delicious."

"Thanks. Are you ready for today?" he asked with a side-eyed glance.

Was she? she wondered. She hoped today would put them one step closer to arresting either one or both of the Konijns and after…

She wouldn't think about the after and possibly finding Isabella and the other women.

"I'm as ready as I'll ever be," she said with a determined nod.

Chapter Nineteen

Diego stood by Ryder and Gabriella as they asked to see the Konijns at the front desk.

The receptionist, the same young woman from the other day, hesitated until the two agents pulled out their badges and held them up for her to see.

With shaky hands, she tapped out a number on her console and as someone answered, she said, "There are two CBI agents here to see you and your father."

The headset kept them from hearing his response, but then the young woman ended the call, rose and walked to the door of the conference room. "They'll be with you shortly."

Barely a minute later, the two Konijns hurried from the far side of the office, their features set in hard, implacable lines.

"If you wouldn't mind stepping inside," she said, and motioned for them to enter.

Before they could, the Konijns stormed up to them.

As Poppy had done the other day, she instantly lay down to notify him that she had scented something. He suspected it was Roberts's scent again.

"This is harassment," Ralph Konijn warned as he pushed past them into the conference room.

The son was slightly more welcoming. "Apologies, but we had to reschedule an important call," Peter said, and swept his hand in the direction of the conference room door.

Gabriella and Ryder walked there, but he hesitated, wondering if he'd pick up on Roberts's scent anywhere else in the office.

At Gabriella's inquiring glance, he pointed to the reception area. "I'll wait out here."

She nodded, hurried into the room and closed the door.

The flustered receptionist wrung her hands nervously. "Is there anything I can get you? Coffee? Tea?" she said, relying on her past training to restore calm.

"Coffee, black, and the men's room would be great," he said with a smile to defuse the awkward situation.

"Restroom is down that corridor and to the right. I'll bring your coffee in a minute," she said, and hurried away from the reception area.

He walked to the end of the corridor, but as he glanced toward the restroom, which he didn't need to use, Poppy jerked him in the opposite direction.

Poppy pulled him along until he reached the large corner office. A plaque identified the space as belonging to Ralph Konijn. She lay down again, confirming she had a scent there.

He clicked his tongue to command her to continue searching and Poppy rose, nosed along the floor until she reached the next office and lay down. Peter's.

He clicked again and Poppy kept going, passing two other offices before she sat down in front of a third. Raul Guarino.

The man came to the door of his office. "May I help you?" he said with an arch of a sandy-colored brow.

"I think I took a wrong turn. I was looking for the restroom," he said, playing dumb.

The man hesitated as if trying to judge if he was telling the truth, but then the receptionist appeared, cradling a cup of coffee.

"I was looking for you. The restrooms are the other way," she said, and shot a worried look at the other man. "I'm so sorry, Mr. Guarino. I should have walked him there."

"Yes, you should have. Make sure it doesn't happen again," he said, chill icicles dripping from his tone.

The receptionist gave him a pleading look. "I'm sorry. I'll just take that coffee and head back to reception to wait for my colleagues," he said, sorry but not sorry that he'd gotten the young woman in trouble.

Poppy had definitely had a hit on Raul Guarino, and he intended to find out why.

GABRIELLA AND RYDER sat opposite the unhappy Konijns.

"As I said before, I consider this police harassment. You have no reason to keep on coming here with all these questions," Ralph said with a dismissive wave of his hand.

"Actually, we have many reasons, but chief among them is finding Jeannie Roberts. And then, arresting a serial killer responsible for the murder of five women," Gabriella said in as calm a tone as she could muster.

Both men jumped a bit, clearly startled.

"Ridiculous," said the elder Konijn.

Peter waved both hands to stop any further questions while at the same time saying, "We have nothing to hide. We've done nothing wrong."

"Both your cellphones were dead around the time of Jeannie's disappearance. How do you explain that?" Ryder pressed.

Father and son shared a look. Peter dipped his head as if pleading with his father to respond and a second later, Ralph said, "We have a secure area at our home for important business discussions. You never know who's listening."

"It's extreme, I know. But we had an important deal go south last year and we suspected that we had been hacked, so we take precautions whenever we can," Peter explained.

Gabriella glanced toward Ryder, thinking it was way too convenient. "And no one can confirm that's where you were at that time?"

"Just my mother. The housekeeper is off on the weekends, and goes home," Peter said.

She suspected she could keep asking questions that wouldn't give them any more information. Because of that, she pushed on to the most important reason they'd come that morning.

"We have DNA evidence that identifies our suspect," she said even though the CSI people were still running the DNA samples through the last of their tests. The initial report had been sent to her just a couple of hours ago.

Both men appeared startled again, and she continued. "We're hoping you'll willingly provide DNA samples so we can eliminate you as suspects," she said as Ryder reached into his jacket pocket to slip on gloves and remove two DNA test kits and evidence bags.

"This is insane," Ralph blustered, but Peter laid a hand on his father's arm to calm him.

"If we do this, will you stop harassing us?" Peter asked.

"No, absolutely not," Ralph interrupted, but once again Peter silenced him with a gentle squeeze of his arm.

"If you have nothing to hide, this is the best way to prove it," Ryder said.

Peter immediately nodded to confirm his acceptance, but Ralph hesitated. At his delay, Peter said, "This is the best way to end this, Father."

With a loud harrumph, Ralph finally relented.

Ryder efficiently opened the first tube, removed the swab and took a sample from Ralph first, obviously worried he'd change his mind.

When he was done, he placed the tube in an evidence bag and marked it with Ralph's name.

He repeated the same procedure with Peter, and once he was done, he tucked the evidence bags into his suit jacket pocket.

"Thank you for your cooperation," Gabriella said, and stood to signal their interview was over.

"We'll keep you advised of any developments," she said, and walked out of the conference room and into the reception area where Diego was sitting, Poppy at his feet.

As soon as he spotted her, he surged to his feet, walked over and leaned close to whisper, "We need to talk."

UPSTAIRS HAD BEEN quiet for hours.

Jeannie assumed he had gone to work much as he had the last few days.

That meant this was her last chance for freedom.

She furiously scraped at the last bolt, trying to remove enough of the crumbling wall to free it as she had the other three bolts.

He hadn't noticed that the night before when he'd come to torment her. She'd been careful to hide the evidence, and he'd seemed distracted as he punished her. Almost as if he was already thinking about the next woman he'd take.

But not if she had anything to say about it.

Today wasn't just about freeing herself. It was about protecting whoever was next.

The plastic spoon snapped from the pressure as she dug it in hard against the wall.

She muttered a curse, but there was no way she'd stop now.

Jerking on the shackles, she felt a little give.

She jerked on it again with just her hands, but it held.

In her brain, she suddenly heard the voice of a former trainer reminding her that her strongest muscles were in her legs.

Lying on her back, she firmly planted her feet on the wall, grabbed the chain with both hands and pulled.

DIEGO WAITED UNTIL they were out the door of the wealth management firm and almost by Gabriella's car to say, "Poppy got a hit on someone else in that office."

She stopped short and whirled to face him. "A hit? Roberts's scent?"

He nodded. "Raul Guarino. He's a few doors down from the Konijns' offices. It could be because of that, but it's worth checking out," he said, sure that it had been more than just possible contamination from the Konijns.

"I'll run him and see what we can find. I'll also share his name with Sophie and Robbie. See what they can come up with," Ryder said, and glanced back toward the office building. "My money is on them being involved in this. I'm hoping the DNA connects them to Isabella's crucifix and that small amount of touch DNA from the first rape/murder."

"I agree. In the meantime, I want to check out some of the locations identified by Wilson's program," Gabriella said, and walked toward her car.

"I'll go with you," Diego said, alert to any possible dangers as he strolled beside her.

As she neared her car, she slowed and then stopped.

Diego wondered why, but then he noticed the envelope tucked beneath the windshield wiper. Again.

Muttering a curse, he shielded her body with his and scrutinized the parking lot. Mostly empty since people had already entered the various buildings since it was past nine o'clock.

"Let me get that," Ryder said, and brushed past them, gloves on and an evidence bag ready to preserve the evidence.

He slipped the envelope from beneath the wiper, opened it and pulled out the single piece of paper within.

A photo of a naked Jeannie Roberts slumped on the ground. Hands and feet shackled to a wall. Above her image in bold black letters: "You're next!"

"Not if I can help it," Diego said, wrapped an arm around Gabriella's waist and tenderly squeezed to offer reassurance.

"If he used a color laser, there may be some hidden metadata in the photo. At a minimum, it should tell us when it was printed," Gabriella said in total investigator mode despite the personal threat.

"Wall and floor look old. It may help us limit which places to visit," Diego said as he scrutinized the other elements in the photo, avoiding the disturbing image of the young woman.

"Let's review the list and start with those older locations," Gabriella said, and glanced at Ryder. "Hopefully CSI can get some prints or touch DNA off the envelope or photo. Compare that to the other samples we have."

"I'll take it straight there. Keep me posted on anything you find at the locations," Ryder said, and marched to his car for the trip to the CBI offices and then Crooked Pass Security.

"Will do," Gabriella said, but her body was tense beneath his hand, a testament to the fact she had been affected by the killer's threat.

Once Ryder was out of earshot, he leaned close and whispered against the side of her face, "Are you okay?"

Chapter Twenty

Am I okay? Gabriella wondered as she battled the visceral reaction to the photo and threat.

"Gabriella?" he pressed at her hesitation.

She set aside her fear and disgust, and strength flooded through her body. Nodding, she said, "I'm more than okay. I'm more determined than ever to stop this guy."

Diego blew out a sigh of relief. "Good. Which location do you want to hit first?"

She opened her car so they could slip inside to review the list.

But as she took a spot behind the wheel as Diego harnessed Poppy and then slipped beside her, she said, "He was here at the same time as us but so were the Konijns. Is it possible that it's not one or both of them?"

"We're letting him track you since you're the bait and it worked. Too well," Diego said.

"The Konijns knew we were here. They may have had time to exit the building, leave this gift for me and still sit for an interview," she said aloud, running through all the possibilities.

"The buildings and parking lot have CCTV. I'll text Sophie and Robbie and have them track that down," Diego said, whipped out his phone and messaged the rest of the CPS team.

While he did that, she reached into the back seat for her briefcase and pulled out the report on the various locations. She opened it on the console so they could review the ages of the sites and visit those that seemed old enough based on what they'd seen in the photo.

They flipped through the pages, identifying likely candidates and once they had those, they mapped out an efficient way to visit them to not waste time.

She just hoped time hadn't run out for Jeannie Roberts.

HIS TRACKER APP beeped to let him know they were on the move.

The tracker had kept him advised so far except for one short blip. He'd worried at the time that it had been found, but since then, it had been working flawlessly.

As he watched where they were going, he breathed a sigh of relief that it wasn't in the direction of his home.

But the fact that they'd come back for another interview warned that he couldn't hold on to Roberts any longer.

He jumped up from his chair, slipped on his winter coat and rushed out a side door much as he had earlier to leave his little gift for Gabriella.

At his car, he hopped in and sped away, eager for those final moments with her. They always brought such satisfaction, as did keeping the right trophy so he could relive the experience until it was time for another woman.

No, not just another woman.

Gabriella.

It would be tough to take her, he thought as he drove.

She always had that muscle-bound gorilla and his dog with her.

Could he take them out first? he wondered, pushing the speed along the mountain roads in his haste to reach Roberts.

His mind raced with all the possibilities, zipping from the pleasure of killing Roberts to how he might get Gabriella alone.

He almost passed the turnoff for his home.

He screeched to a stop and backed up to make the turn.

Loose gravel kicked up as he sped along the road leading to his home.

But when he neared the house, a slight motion in the woods snagged his attention.

Roberts. Running through the underbrush.

He cursed, jammed on the brakes and threw his door open to chase after her.

Fear stopped her cold as she heard a car gunning up the drive.

Jeannie hadn't expected him home so soon.

She'd thought she'd have hours to find a way back to a main road and hopefully salvation.

Past the underbrush and trees with their first blasts of spring green, she detected a silver-gray Range Rover racing up the road.

She should have moved deep into the woods and away from the driveway, but it had been the only guide to finding civilization. The home where she was being held was fairly remote and although she'd spotted a house farther up the mountain, she'd decided heading down to a main road might be better than a house that might be a vacation home.

As he flung his door open and flew out, intending to recapture her, she caught her first glimpse of his face.

Handsome. Sandy-haired. Familiar, she realized, but couldn't place him.

She memorized that face, because when she made it to freedom, he'd pay for what he'd done.

Armed with that thought, she raced through the underbrush as he came after her.

Gabriella put an X through the third location on their list and sighed.

It had been nearly two hours since they'd left the Konijns'

offices to visit the homes they'd identified based on the photo the killer had left behind.

The photo with the "You're next" had rattled through her brain over and over as they'd inspected each of the locations.

There had been cooperative residents at two locations who had let them walk Poppy around and were only too willing to help.

But that kind of help didn't eliminate them immediately. It wasn't unusual for criminals to appear eager as a ruse.

No one had been home at the third location, but Diego had walked Poppy around the front porch area and door. She hadn't scented anything, and so they'd decided to move on.

"This home is farther than I thought," she said as she drove to the mountainside location.

"It'll take at least twenty minutes," he said with a wry grin.

She chuckled and shook her head. "At least."

A second later, her cell phone rang with an incoming call. Ryder.

She hoped he had good news for them.

"What do you have?" she asked as she turned onto the highway for the ride to the fourth location.

"They've finished processing the DNA test kits and are working to compare them to the DNA we have from Isabella's crucifix, the touch DNA and CODIS. That may take another hour or so," he advised. In the background, there was suddenly loud talking and the sounds of activity.

"Hold on," Ryder said, and appeared to be speaking to someone before coming back on the line.

"We just heard from a local police department that they have Jack Hayes in custody. It was a routine traffic stop and when the officer checked, he realized there was a BOLO."

"Great. Text me their address and we'll head there after our next stop," she said, and did a side-eyed glance at Diego who nodded to confirm that course of action.

"I'll head there now and wait for you," Ryder said, and ended the call.

"What do you think Hayes will add to this investigation?" Diego asked, eyes narrowed as he examined her.

She did a little shrug. "I don't know. It almost feels like a diversion."

"I agree," he said with a nod.

"A diversion that's costing us time," she lamented, reminded yet again of the clock that was ticking.

"Do you think his threats are a diversion also?" Diego wondered aloud.

"Bringing Isabella into the mix is a bigger distraction. He has to know how much it means to me to find her," she said, and hesitated, dipping her head from side to side before tacking on, "I'm not sure I take the threats seriously."

"I take them seriously. Very seriously," he said, and brushed the back of his hand along her cheek.

She smiled, appreciating his concerns. "Thank you, but think about it. He has to get past you and Poppy. Not an easy task," she said, and pulled over for the exit to a smaller road that ran along the base of the mountain.

"Not an easy task," he admitted as she glanced at Poppy, who was perched on the back seat, watching the world go by.

A world that wasn't going by fast enough, she thought and increased her speed in her haste to reach the next location and then head to the local police station to interview Hayes.

Luckily, there was little traffic on the side road, and in no time, she was traveling up the mountainside. She was about halfway when she had to slow to search for the turnoff for the location.

"Seems remote," she said as she turned onto a gravel driveway.

"Remote is good for lots of reasons, but especially for a serial killer. But it's a pricey location for someone who we think is what? Twentysomething?" he said as he glanced around the area.

"Not if you're born with a silver spoon like Peter Konijn or his father," she said, and did a final turn to pull in front of a large contemporary home with soaring windows that provided views of the nearby mountains as well as the city of Denver.

They exited the car and approached the front door. She rang the doorbell, but no one answered. She had expected as much since there was no car in the driveway, although one could have been parked in the nearby three-car garage.

Shaking her head, she said, "This is so wrong. This is not the kind of home we expected. It's not old at all."

"No, but maybe it's been renovated and sits on the foundation of an older home," Diego said as he stepped back off the porch to examine the structure.

His perusal was interrupted by the crunch of gravel as a vehicle came up the path.

A delivery truck.

The driver pulled behind them, got out and then walked up with a package.

"Are you Peter Konijn?" he asked, and even before Diego answered, he was handing the package to him.

"Thanks, but I'm not. Do you do regular deliveries here?" Diego asked.

The driver nodded. "He does a lot of online shopping."

The driver's eyes narrowed then, and he skipped his gaze from him to Poppy, and then to Gabriella. "You cops?"

Gabriella flashed her badge. "Yes, why?"

With a big shift of his shoulders, he said, "No reason, except, it's just weird I've never seen him in the four years I've been on this route. Even when I ring and know that someone's home, he never comes to the door. Never leaves a holiday tip either, when he has the money to build this big fancy house." He tossed his hand in the direction of the home with a harrumph.

"Were you on the route before he built this house?" Gabriella asked.

The driver nodded. "I was. It used to be an old cabin. They tore it down."

And built the big fancy home over an old foundation and possibly a cellar, Diego thought.

"Do you remember when he did that?" Gabriella asked, and Diego immediately knew where she was going.

The driver pursed his lips and looked upward as he considered when that might have happened. "About two years ago. It took them a while to finish the new place. Just completed it a couple of months ago."

"Thanks. I'm going to give you my business card in case you think of anything else," Gabriella said.

The driver took the card, did a jaunty little salute and then returned to his truck to resume his delivery route.

Diego held the package in his hands and glanced at the name again just to confirm. With a dip of his head, he said, "This isn't the address we have for Peter, but he could use this as a vacation home. Plus, there's this: two years to build. Two years with no kidnappings, right?"

"Two years between the Nations and Cornerstone kidnappings and Roberts's disappearance. That's just too much coincidence. Let's have Poppy scent the front door," she said.

Diego followed as she walked to the door, Poppy at his side. At the door, he instructed her to scent all around, but she didn't indicate that she had a scent. He pondered that for a moment, and then said, "If Roberts was wrapped up in something, like a blanket, and carried…"

He hesitated because even with that, Poppy should have picked up on a scent unless…

Bending low and close to the ground, where large slabs of slate sat close to the home, he inhaled deeply.

A perfumy fragrance mixed with the stronger aroma of a bleachy substance.

Standing once again, he pointed along the edge of the home and said, "It's been cleaned with something that might be throwing off Poppy. Let me walk her around the house and see if she picks up on anything."

She nodded, and he forged ahead, brushing through some decorative bushes by the side of the house. They had just been planted judging from the fresh earth and stakes a landscaper had put to hold them in place until they rooted.

At his command, Poppy sniffed along the edges of the home, nose to the ground.

Nothing happened until they reached the back corner of the home. At that point, Poppy lay down to confirm she had a scent.

"Good girl," Diego said and fed her a treat. "*Such*," he said, instructing Poppy to continue her search.

Poppy immediately shot to her feet, but seemed conflicted as to which direction to go, almost as if she was catching a scent in either direction. "*Such*," he said, and guided her toward the back of the home.

Poppy eagerly took off in that direction, stopped by a sliding glass door and lay down.

He was about to reach for the door when Gabriella laid a hand on his arm to stop him. "We don't have a warrant and probably not enough probable cause at this point. If we go in, we risk jeopardizing evidence."

He muttered a silent curse, worried that Roberts might still be inside. But then it occurred to him that Poppy had a hit away from the house as well.

Gesturing back toward the corner of the home, he said, "Poppy picked up a scent there also. If Roberts was able to escape…"

"Let's see what's there," she said, and they walked back in

that direction. As they neared the corner, Gabriella gestured to the imprint of a boot print.

Diego bent slightly to examine it. "Looks familiar. Like what we found at the scout camp."

Gabriella nodded. "Definitely. If Roberts escaped, Peter might have been right on her trail."

He muttered a curse, straightened and instructed Poppy to continue her search.

His canine pushed on, nose to the ground, and they followed, careful to look for more boot prints.

They were about fifteen yards from the house and halfway to the road when they noticed an area where the leaves and underbrush had been disturbed. Carefully they made their way toward it. Poppy yanked to go to the area where a scuffle had clearly occurred.

The German shepherd lay down and Diego rewarded her with a head rub. "Good girl," he said as he stood to examine the ground.

"If she escaped, she didn't get far," he said, and glanced back to the house.

Gabriella peered down the mountainside. "Just a little farther and she would have gotten to the road. Someone might have seen her there."

He didn't doubt it, but based on the disturbance before them, Roberts had been taken again.

"My gut says she's not here anymore," he said, doing a slow turn on his heel to scrutinize the area all around them.

"I agree, but if she's not here, she's likely dead," Gabriella said with a disgusted sigh, and jammed her hands on her hips as she also did a slow perusal of the location.

But then she was in action, whipping out her cell phone and calling Ryder. When he answered, she said, "We need to bring in Peter Konijn and we need a warrant."

Chapter Twenty-One

To avoid wasting time, Ryder brought Peter Konijn and his blustering father to the same police station where Jack Hayes was being held.

When Gabriella arrived with Diego and Poppy, Ryder guided them to a conference room. Once they were inside, he said, "Peter Konijn has lawyered up. We're waiting for the lawyer to arrive, so I thought we'd start with Jack Hayes. See what we get from him."

Gabriella nodded. "Any news on the DNA matches or the warrant?"

"The request for the warrant was prepared and I have an agent going to a friendly judge to sign it. As for the DNA matches, I'm told any minute now," he advised.

"Great. Progress," she said although in her heart she worried it was possibly too late for Jeannie Roberts.

Ryder held his hand out in the direction of a nearby interrogation room.

"I'm going to hang back. I want to reach out to Sophie and Robbie and see if they have anything. Plus, I should walk Poppy," Diego said.

Ryder nodded. "Just ask the officers to let you in when you're done."

Gabriella walked to the door and waited for Ryder, and then the two of them entered the interview room.

As soon as she did, she knew Hayes was not the man who

had been lurking around the CPS offices. He was too tall and as heavily muscled as a professional wrestler. Also, he had very obvious tattoos on his hands and fingers, and as she dug up her memories from the video feeds they had, she didn't recall any such visible markings.

But as those seconds in the parking garage flashed through her mind, she could picture him as the man at the wheel. She hadn't seen much past the tinted window and the muzzle fire, but she had seen that he was tall.

"Jack Hayes. I'm CBI Agent Gabriella Ruiz and this is CBI Agent Ryder Hunt," she said as she sat down, and Ryder handed her a file.

She opened the file and skimmed through the long rap sheet. "Drug dealing, assault, burglary, and now we can add attempted murder and federal gun violations."

He sat there sullenly, powerful hands clasped before him. Head downturned to look at the hands shackled to the table.

"I don't think you did this on your own," Gabriella began. "I think someone paid you to shoot us. I think Peter Konijn paid you."

A burst of laughter escaped him. "Rabbit? You think I'd tell you if Rabbit paid me?" he said with another laugh and abrupt shake of his head.

"Rabbit? You call him 'Rabbit'?" Ryder pressed.

Hayes finally looked up, obviously amused. "Yeah. That's what we used to call him in college."

"Why?" Gabriella asked, wondering why anyone would give him a nickname that made him sound like a child's storybook character.

With a lift of his heavily muscled shoulders, he explained. "We had a Dutch exchange student who told us Konijn meant 'rabbit.' And boy was he that in college with the girls," he said and made a crude hand gesture.

Gabriella shared a look of disgust with Ryder before proceeding. "You obviously know Rabbit quite well. So maybe you know that he's possibly murdered some women. Women you might know," she said, pulled some photos from her file and placed them in front of Hayes.

She tapped the first photo. "Alyssa Nations. She went to college with you, too. She's been missing for over two years."

She did the same with the second photo, tapping Cornerstone's photo. "Missy's been missing about the same time. We assume that both of them are dead and that your friend Rabbit is responsible."

Without missing a beat, she removed Roberts's photo and laid it before him. "We also think he took this woman and is about to murder her."

That shrug came again, along with a negligent toss of his head. "What's that got to do with me?"

"Are you familiar with the felony murder rule?" she asked.

"Do I look like a lawyer?" Hayes blurted out with a sarcastic laugh and jerk of his body.

It was as good a time as any for the good cop, bad cop routine. Looking at Ryder, she said, "I'll let my colleague explain."

Ryder nodded. "We don't like accomplices in Colorado. We think they're as responsible for a death as much as the person who pulled the trigger," he began, but Hayes didn't respond so he continued.

"Being an accomplice means not just taking part in the murder. It also means in the furtherance of the act. Do you know what that means? In the furtherance of?" Ryder pressed.

He was met with silence again, so he explained. "That means helping him in any way. That includes trying to kill Gabriella and our civilian consultant in that parking lot to keep us from investigating those murders and the kidnapping."

"I have nothing to do with any of that," Hayes said as it finally registered that he might be in deep trouble.

"Once we prove Rabbit is responsible, you'll go down with

him, which could get you anywhere from sixteen to forty-eight years in prison. I'm going to ask the judge to give you that for each of these women," Ryder said, and jabbed a finger on the women's photos.

Hayes jumped to life, surging up in his chair and slamming his hands on the tabletop. "I have nothing to do with this."

"But you do according to the felony murder rule, Jack. Your good friend Rabbit just ended your life unless you cooperate," Gabriella said in a soothing tone, wanting to cajole Hayes into assisting them.

"Cooperate? How?" he asked, his earlier sullen behavior fading.

"Admit that Rabbit hired you and why. Tell us what you know about these women," Gabriella said, and held her hand palm upward in an invitation for him to speak.

"You'll go to bat for me?" he asked, his blue-eyed gaze almost pleading.

"We'll speak to the district attorney about your cooperation," Gabriella said.

Hayes hesitated, but with a rush of breath, he said, "Rabbit came to me. Said some people were hassling him and he needed someone to warn them off."

"He asked you to shoot at us?" Gabriella asked, just to make sure she understood what Peter Konijn had asked him to do.

Hayes shook his head. "He didn't tell me how. He just wanted me to scare you off. I figured a drive-by might do it, but I only meant to scare you."

He had accomplished that, not that she would admit it.

"He thought scaring us would stop our investigation?" Ryder asked with an abrupt laugh.

"You'd have to ask him," Hayes said, and shrugged those powerful shoulders again.

"We will, Jack. We have Rabbit in a room just a few doors down," Gabriella said, and stood.

Ryder did the same and said, "An officer will be in to take you back to the jail."

Without another word, they exited and met for a second in the hall before entering the second interview room where the Konijns waited.

"Not the sharpest tack," Ryder said.

Gabriella couldn't disagree. "Peter isn't either if he thought he could scare us off."

"Stupid move," Ryder said.

They were about to walk to the other interview room a few doors down when an officer entered the area followed by an older man in an expensive three-piece pin-striped suit and shiny black oxford shoes.

The Konijns' lawyer, she supposed, which was confirmed as he walked past them and into the interview room, briefcase in hand.

"Looks expensive," Ryder said.

"Looks like we'll have a tough time, but I'm good to go," Gabriella said, and Ryder echoed it.

"I'm good. Let's go," she said, and walked into the interview room.

DIEGO KNEW HE had no place in the interview room. He wasn't a cop, after all.

But he also couldn't just sit there being useless.

He called Sophie and Robbie, hoping they had been able to get additional information.

When Sophie answered, he said, "Tell me you have something."

"We do. We were able to clean up the license on that Range Rover enough to get a hit and no surprise, it's part of a fleet rented out to one of the shell companies we believe are owned by the Konijns. We're sending you the info," Robbie said, and a second later, the whoosh of his phone confirmed he'd gotten a message.

Sophie continued with their report. "We couldn't get any help on the lidar front, so we tried another route. Wilson was able to get satellite images of the area over several years in and around the disappearance of Nations and Cornerstone."

"The images were that clear?" he asked, wondering what they could see from thousands of miles in space.

"He reached out to a friend in NASA. They have the Worldview website, which is a real-time satellite map, but its resolution isn't very sharp. But they have other images that are high-res, and he was able to process them," Sophie advised.

The whoosh said Sophie had sent those images.

"Wilson has identified some spots above the scout camp that warrant investigation," Sophie added.

"Great. That's a lot of useful information," he said.

"We've got more," Robbie said, excitement in his voice.

"Hit me with it," he said, also growing excited that they finally had more to work with.

"We have this morning's CCTV video from the Konijns' parking lot. The good news is that we have video of someone approaching Gabriella's car. Based on the time stamp, it could be Peter Konijn. The bad news is that the video is very poor quality. But we were able to enhance it," Robbie said, and the whoosh that followed had him glancing at the image of their suspect.

Even enhanced the image was grainy. "It could be Peter Konijn," he said, but wondered if that was being influenced by all the other evidence they'd gathered so far.

"We ran Peter's photo to compare and got a match, but then again, with an image this grainy it could just be someone who looks similar," Sophie said, the earlier excitement fading.

"It's something, though," he said to offer his team encouragement.

"We'll keep pushing and see what else we can find," Sophie said.

"Thank you. This is all good."

He took a quick look at the information they'd sent, but since he'd always been better on his feet, he decided to take another walk with Poppy, who was always grateful for the activity.

Heading out of the precinct again, he let Poppy take the lead, strolling along the street as he considered the information CPS had provided, especially the comparisons of the satellite images of the scout camp area.

There had been more than just three areas flagged on that mountainside.

Did that mean that in addition to Isabella, Cornerstone and Nations there were others?

And what about the two other women who didn't fit the MO of the serial killer but had been identified by Wilson's program?

They had yet to do an in-depth review of those cases, but he suspected that if they were able to prove Konijn was their man, they could pull all the evidence from those crimes and tie him to those rapes and murders as well. Especially since they'd found some touch DNA at the first scene that hadn't been noticed before.

Which had him wondering what was going on in those interrogation rooms.

Turning, he gave Poppy one last chance to relieve herself, cleaned and then hurried back to the precinct.

THE KONIJNS SAT at the interview table flanked by their high-priced attorney, who handed them a business card as soon as they entered.

Before they were even in their seats, the attorney said, "I strenuously object to your treatment of my clients."

"Mr. Bruce. To be clear, your clients are implicated in the

disappearance, and likely murder, of three women, and the rape and murder of two other women," Gabriella said.

Ryder immediately jumped in. "And the kidnapping and imminent murder of Jeannie Roberts."

"My clients strongly deny those allegations," Bruce said, his tone as unctuous as the gel keeping every strand of hair in place.

"We also have proof that Rabbit," she began and looked in Peter's direction. "That is your nickname, isn't it, Peter? Rabbit?" she repeated just to embarrass him some more.

It worked as his face flushed and he angrily tapped the tabletop with his fingers as he slouched in his seat.

"Your friend, Jack Hayes, who's in a room just a few doors down, shot at me and a civilian consultant. He's indicated that you hired him to scare us off," Gabriella said.

Ralph Konijn surprised them by looking at his son and blurting out, "Jack Hayes. That idiot friend?"

The color on Peter's face deepened to almost maroon, and that nervous tap grew ever faster.

"Peter? Answer me," Ralph said, and at that, his attorney laid a hand on his arm to silence him.

"My clients need a moment. Alone," Bruce said.

"Not a problem but while you're at it, you may want to explain to Ralph about the felony murder rule," she said as a parting shot.

When she exited the room, Ryder at her back, she realized Diego was standing just a few feet away, head buried in his phone, and Poppy at his feet.

As he noticed them, he looked up and smiled. It warmed her inside and awoke a wealth of emotions.

"How's it going?" he asked.

"Ralph Konijn is being as overbearing as usual but that might work to our advantage. Jack Hayes fingered Peter as the person who hired him to shoot at us. No pun intended, but that gives us a lot of ammunition," Gabriella said.

"Big pun," he said with a grin.

She pointed to his phone. "Do you have anything?"

He held up a photo for them to see. "This was taken from the Konijns' parking lot. Based on the time stamp, Peter could have gone to your car before he joined you in the conference room."

"Fuzzy. It could be Peter or someone who looks like him," Ryder said as he bent slightly to examine the photo.

"CPS is going to use facial recognition software to see if it helps at all," he said and quickly added, "But there's more."

Gabriella watched as he pulled up another image of a mountainside marked with an assortment of circles. "Is that the scout camp area?" she asked.

"It is, and those circles are changes in the topography based on comparisons of satellite imagery over the years," he explained.

Ryder narrowed his gaze and asked, "Changes? Natural or—"

"Likely man-made. We'll have to take Poppy there to see what she can find," he said, and swiped his phone closed.

"That's all we have so far," he said with an almost disappointed tone.

She cupped his jaw and stroked her thumb along his chin. "It's all helpful."

The door to the interview room opened then, and the attorney poked his head out and said, "My client wishes to speak to you."

Chapter Twenty-Two

Gabriella and Ryder reentered the interview room and sat but before they could say a word, the attorney raised his hand.

"Before we proceed, we need to discuss what you can do for my clients in exchange for their cooperation," Bruce said.

"That depends on the information that your clients are willing to provide," Gabriella advised, hopeful that Peter would confess where he had taken Jeannie Roberts.

"We'd want a reduced sentence for cooperation," Bruce said with a nervous glance at his clients.

Ryder, still in bad cop mode, jumped in. "You want a reduced sentence for no less than three murders, possibly five, and the latest kidnapping?"

Peter waved his hands in the air in denial and said, "I have nothing to do with what happened to those women."

Gabriella gave the attorney a laser-like stare. "Doesn't sound like cooperation to me."

"As Mr. Konijn has said, he has nothing to do with those murders or the kidnapping," Bruce said calmly.

Her gut told her something wasn't adding up. As Ryder started to say something, she stuck out her hand to ask him to wait. "If Peter isn't going to confess to these murders and the kidnapping—"

"I'm not. I have nothing to do with them," Peter insisted yet again.

Gabriella and Ryder shared a glance, and then she faced the attorney and asked, "What is your client willing to plead to?"

"In connection with the shooting that took place, my client is willing to plead guilty to misdemeanor menacing—"

"Menacing with a deadly weapon is a felony demanding jail time and fines," Gabriella countered.

"No jail time, but we're willing to pay a reasonable fine," Bruce advised after a quick look at Ralph Konijns, who had sat there, stone-faced, ever since they had reentered. His usual bluster was gone, replaced by simmering anger.

It was apparent in the flush across his face, the tight lines of his body and how his hands were clasped so tightly before him that his fingers were white from the pressure.

She was angry as well that Bruce and the Konijns thought they could get away with the murders thanks to their money.

That anger made her shoot to her feet. "Peter Konijn. We're arresting you for the murder of Isabella Ruiz and the attempted murders of myself and civilian consultant Diego Rodriguez," she said since so far, they only had DNA for Isabella's murder and Hayes's confession about the shooting.

Peter and his attorney immediately protested, but she ignored the protest as Ryder stood, handcuffs in hand, and approached Peter. "Please rise, hands behind your back."

Grudgingly, Peter complied, still protesting as Gabriella read him his Miranda rights and asked him if he understood those rights.

"Of course I do. I'm not an idiot," he said but lost some of that confidence as Ryder walked him to the door.

"Dad, do something," Peter pleaded, and looked back at his father.

Ralph Konijn only shook his head, looked away and mumbled, "My sons are idiots."

She should have been shocked by his lack of care, but then

again, he struck her as the kind of man who only cared about himself and how people would perceive him.

The attorney jumped to his feet. "We will get you out of here, Peter. I'll speak to a judge immediately."

Gabriella followed Ryder and Peter out of the room and walked with them to the jail portion of the precinct where Jack Hayes was sitting in one of the cells. The last thing they wanted was to put Peter nearby so the two men could cook up some kind of lie, so Ryder walked him to a cell at the far end and secured him there, ignoring him as he continued to protest his innocence.

As they were walking to where Diego waited for them with Poppy, Ryder said, "Methinks he doth protest too much."

"He does, but something is bothering me," she said, and stopped as Diego and Poppy joined them.

"What's wrong?" Diego said, and stroked a hand down her arm, mindful of not having a big PDA in front of Ryder and all the police officers in the area.

"My gut tells me we're missing something," she said, shook her head and then said, "Did you hear what Ralph said as we were walking out?"

Ryder frowned and shrugged. "About his son being an idiot?"

"Sons. I think he said 'sons' but as far as we know, he has only one," Gabriella advised, and glanced toward the cell where Peter was now pacing back and forth nervously.

The whoosh of an incoming message erupted from Ryder's phone, delaying discussion.

He glanced at the message, muttered a curse and then jerked his head in the direction of a nearby conference room.

Once they were inside, he handed the phone to Gabriella.

"The DNA doesn't belong to either Peter or Ralph Konijns. But it does belong to a close family member. Plus, it's a match to the new touch DNA evidence found at the home of one of the other murder victims," she said.

"A family member?" Diego pressed.

Gabriella nodded. "Yes, a family member. I'm sure he said 'sons.'"

"Let's replay the tape and confirm," Ryder said, and hurried from the room to obtain a copy of the recording, leaving Gabriella and Diego alone in the room.

Gabriella's upset was obvious and with Ryder gone, Diego didn't hesitate to cup her cheek and offer comfort.

"We were so sure it was Peter and now this," she said, distressed.

"But you were on the right trail. It is a Konijn. Just not one we know about," Diego reassured her.

"Ralph could be an illegitimate son. Why doesn't that surprise me? He's so…arrogant. He thinks rules don't apply to him, even the rules about being faithful to your spouse," she said angrily.

Ryder returned a second later, a USB drive in hand that he placed into a nearby computer to bring up the recording. He fast-forwarded to the moment just before Gabriella had indicated that they would be arresting Peter.

The video played and Ralph's words echoed in the room.

"My sons are idiots."

For good measure, Ryder rewound the tape and played it a second time.

"My sons are idiots."

"We need to bring Ralph back in," Gabriella said, pulled out the attorney's business card and dialed the number.

There was an angry burst from the man that even Diego could hear. "This is harassment. We've only just left the station."

"Then we'll expect you to come in soon," she said, and ended the call.

"Gutsy," Diego said in approval.

Gabriella smiled. "I don't expect Ralph is going to be forthcoming about any of his affairs. Do you think Crooked Pass Security can do anything with these DNA results?"

"Possibly. Genetic genealogy can trace ancestry and relationships between people, but that can take time," he said.

"Whatever you can do would be appreciated," Ryder said, and immediately sent the DNA results to Sophie.

Almost instantly another whoosh sounded, and Ryder said, "Bruce and Ralph Konijn are back. An officer is taking them back to the interview room."

"We should go," she said but then faced Diego. "I just hate wasting your time by having you just sit here."

"If you don't mind, I'd like to watch the interview. I'm a pretty good judge of character and after, I'd like to go to the scout camp and check out the anomalies on those satellite images," Diego said.

"I'll arrange for that," Ryder said, and left the room.

"You should go. We can meet you there," she said, worry darkening her gaze.

He should, but he was worried about what they might find, and as difficult as it might be, Gabriella should be there if he found Isabella.

"I thought you might want to be there in case..."

He didn't need to finish. With a nod, she said, "I want to be there."

Since they were in the conference room, he didn't hesitate to bring her close and hug her hard, offering comfort.

When she pulled away, she swiped at the tears on her face and with a deep inhale, prepared herself for the upcoming interview.

A knock at the door came only a second before Ryder walked in. "We're ready."

They walked out of the room, and Ryder directed Diego to an observation area behind the interview room. As he entered, he noted that Ralph Konijn and the attorney were seated at the table, heads bent close, whispering to each other until Gabriella and Ryder walked in.

Immediately they sat up and became silent.

Gabriella and Ryder sat across from them, and Gabriella said, "We now have DNA results that confirm your son committed the abduction and murder of Isabella Ruiz and the rape and murder of Sadie Lyons."

A bit of a stretch since all they knew was that it was a family member, but based on Konijn's earlier words, logical.

"Peter did not do that," Ralph calmly said.

"You're right. It wasn't Peter. It was your other son. Would you care to share more info about him?" she asked.

Ralph would be good at poker, Diego thought, since the man had no response to Gabriella's words other than to deny it.

"Peter is my only son."

"Not true. DNA doesn't lie, and I can understand why you'd deny it. I'm sure your wife and colleagues would be appalled to find out you have an illegitimate son. Especially one who's a serial killer," Gabriella said, and then reached into the file before her.

She withdrew a photo. The contemporary home they had visited about two hours earlier.

"Nice house, right? Replaced an old cabin that used to be there," she said, and at that, a slight tic jumped along Ralph's jaw.

"We expect to have a warrant any minute now to search that home. I think what we'll find is more DNA and enough evidence to connect your son to five—" she held up one hand in the air, fingers spread "—that's five murders that could become six if you don't help us."

"I have no other son," he said, but his voice this time was a little shaky and that tic in his jaw only grew jumpier.

Gabriella sighed and leaned back in her chair. "Mr. Bruce,"

she said, and faced the attorney. "I hope you did what I asked and explained the felony murder rule to your client."

"I did, Agent Ruiz. By the way, is it a coincidence you have the same name as the first alleged victim or do you have a connection and conflict?" he asked smoothly.

"Isabella was—is—my little sister. You might think that's a conflict, maybe because it makes me even more determined," she said.

The attorney glanced at Ryder and said, "Highly irregular, wouldn't you say? This kind of connection could bias this agent against my client."

Diego held his breath, knowing that Ryder hadn't necessarily agreed with Gabriella's theories about the cases, even though they'd proven to be accurate. For all Diego knew, Ryder had also had qualms about Gabriella being too personally involved.

"My colleague has been totally professional in her handling of this case. I have no doubt anyone reviewing it will confirm that. I also do not doubt that we will prove your client's illegitimate son is responsible for these horrible crimes," he said, and then flipped a hand in the direction of Ralph Konijn.

"Your client, on the other hand, has done nothing but obstruct the investigation. He knows who owns this house," he said, and pointedly jabbed a finger at the photo.

"He knows his illegitimate son owns it. He may even know what his son has been doing, which makes him responsible for these murders," Ryder said, and opened his copy of the file and yanked out photos of the murdered women.

For emphasis, he pointed a finger at Isabella's photo and said, "Isabella was only twelve. Twelve."

A change came over Ralph Konijn then as he glanced from Isabella's photo to Gabriella. It was almost like watching the Grinch develop a heart, something he hadn't thought possible with the arrogant and uncaring Konijn.

"I'm sorry this happened to your family," he said, and then bent and whispered something in his attorney's ear.

"We need a few minutes," Bruce said.

Gabriella and Ryder immediately left the room, and Diego joined them in the hallway.

"He's going to talk," he said, having witnessed what he thought was a transformation of the older Konijn.

"I think so. That'll give us a name, probably faster than we would have had with genetic genealogy. But it's just a name," Gabriella said in a tone that was part exhausted and part disappointed.

Barely a minute later, Bruce opened the door to the interview room and called out, "My client wishes to speak to you."

Chapter Twenty-Three

The air vibrated around him, alive with the signs of spring and something else.

Danger.

As wide-open as the spaces were around him as he carried Jeannie's limp body up the trail, the world felt like it was closing in around him.

The agents were close. Through the video cameras he'd set up in and around his home, he'd seen them poking around. And a couple of hours later, he'd seen the CSI truck pull up.

He did not doubt they'd gotten a warrant and would be ransacking his home for evidence. It might take them a little time to find the entrance to the cellar, but they'd find it. And when they did…

He had thought about running, and as he trudged up to the scout camp, he thought about it again.

It wasn't too late to empty the rest of the money in his bank accounts into a Swiss account he'd opened years earlier. It was enough money to sustain him for years. Certainly enough to buy him a fake identity.

But running struck him as the coward's way out.

It felt wrong.

What felt right was vengeance. Retribution for ruining the life he had built for himself.

All would still be great if it wasn't for that persistent CBI agent.

That beautiful CBI agent, he thought, recalling what he'd seen of her when she'd come to interview his father and half brother.

Isabella had been beautiful as well. And innocent. So innocent.

His first in so many ways. He realized Roberts wasn't meant to be his last.

No, Gabriella had to be his last.

Jeannie moaned as he dumped her in a corner of the room in one of the last remaining structures at the scout camp. This shower room was farther up the mountain, well removed from where he had taken Isabella, and not as well-known. It was from an earlier embodiment of the camp that had been abandoned for the location lower down the mountain.

Jeannie moved and moaned again as she lay against the wooden wall.

Good. The ketamine was wearing off.

He squatted there, watching her awaken. Watching that lovely fear in her eyes and then the determination.

Standing, he took out the knife and held it up for her to see.

Her eyes opened wide, and she struggled against the bindings at her hands and feet, not that she'd be able to escape.

Lifting his cell phone, he recorded her struggles, pleased by them. Growing aroused as well, but he fought back desire.

He had to stay clearheaded if he was going to exact precious vengeance.

Satisfied he had enough video, he slipped his knife into a sheath at his waist and walked out of the shower stalls.

Cell service was weak here. He'd have to climb farther up the mountainside, which was fine.

It would be the perfect spot for all this to end.

But first, he had to leave his little surprise for whoever might find Roberts. He'd been working on it for a week or so from plans on the internet, but he hadn't had a chance to test it yet.

Still, he did not doubt he had done it right and would accomplish the job.

Hiking up the mountain, he found the perfect spot and took a moment to appreciate the views of the valley below and then his killing fields, recalling the spots where he had placed Isabella and the others. So many others.

Smiling, he brought up the video and edited it to a perfect section. Then he typed out a message, marked his location with a pin and sent the video.

Then he sat down to wait for her.

Raul Guarino.

Gabriella was familiar with the name since Diego had mentioned Poppy getting a hit on the man at the Konijns' wealth management firm.

"Raul is Ralph in Italian. His mother must have named him that to either honor or goad Konijn," Gabriella said.

"He lived in that cabin with his mother. Konijn said he paid for it and that he would visit off and on until Raul became a teen and his mother died. Then things got tense between them," Gabriella said, recalling Konijn's earlier testimony.

"He may have felt abandoned when she died and angry when his father tried to keep him under his thumb the way he does Peter," Diego said.

"But he brought him into the firm," Ryder said, head slightly downturned as he considered all that Konijn had revealed during the interrogation.

"Possibly to keep him silent about the affair," Gabriella suggested.

"That tension that he mentioned happened right around when Isabella disappeared and with his mother's death, he had that cabin all to himself," Diego said, and it made her heart ache at the thought of Isabella all alone in that cabin cellar, suffering at Guarino's hands.

Diego picked up on her upset since he stroked a hand down her arm, tenderly held her hand and offered a reassuring squeeze.

"Don't think about it," he said, aware that she was hurting.

"Tough to do," she admitted with a strangled sigh.

A sudden whoosh of a message intruded.

Ryder slipped his phone from his pocket and smiled as he read the message. "They're executing the warrant. They'll keep me posted on any developments."

"Great," she said, and was about to discuss their next steps when her phone made the familiar doorbell chime that said she also had a message.

It was from an unknown number with no preview to hint at the content.

She almost deleted it, thinking it might be spam, but with everything going on, she didn't want to miss any message that might help with the investigation.

But as the video played, it took all her strength to stay on her feet as her blood ran cold and her heart seemed to stop beating in her chest.

Diego laid a hand on her arm as she wavered and with a shaky hand, she shared the message with them.

THE HEAT OF anger tangled with fear in his gut as he viewed Jeannie Roberts, tied up like a hog for slaughter, with the bright red word "Trade?" across the top of the video. As he tamed his anger, he realized there was also a pin location in the message text.

"Trade? Does he seriously think we'd trade you for Roberts?" he said, disbelief in his tone.

"We need to see where this is," Gabriella said, and tapped the pin to reveal the location.

Diego immediately recognized the area. It was high up on the mountain where the scout camp was located.

"He's gone to his killing fields," he said, worried about what that might mean for both Roberts and Gabriella.

"I don't think this pin is for Roberts," Ryder said as he also examined the location revealed by the pin.

"I agree. This is where he is. Where he wants to meet me," Gabriella said.

Diego's gut tightened again at the thought of her offering herself for their victim. "No way. You can't do that. He's too dangerous."

"We've been having a cold snap. It's barely past forty and Roberts can't last for long, even if she is in some kind of shelter," Gabriella warned, and glanced at the video again. "Do you think this is one of the buildings at the scout camp?"

Diego examined the dingy wood in the video. "Possibly," he said, and worried about the gaps between the wooden planks on the floor and walls, which would let cold into the space.

"We need to see how to approach this location," Gabriella said, and then hurried back into the nearby conference room.

Ryder and Diego followed, Poppy at his side.

Gabriella grabbed her laptop from her knapsack and a second later, broadcast the image of the location on a nearby monitor.

"I've never been up in this area when I was a scout. It's challenging to reach the summit," she said, rose and gestured to the area identified by the pin.

"But Roberts is not there. He's trying to distract from where he's hidden Roberts," Diego said.

"Do you think that you and Poppy can follow Roberts's scent and find her?" she said.

He didn't doubt it, but it might take time, especially if this building was farther up the mountain.

"Can you overlay those satellite images that Sophie and Robbie got for us?" he said, hoping they'd help limit the search area.

"I might not be a tech genius, but I think I can manage that," she said, and a few minutes later, she had dropped the image over the pin, sized it, and increased the transparency so they could see the location of the pin as well as the anomalies identified by Sophie and Robbie's analysis.

Diego walked to the monitor, jammed his hands on his hips and examined the images. Ryder joined him there, also scrutinizing the area.

"Guarino is almost at the summit. You said you've never been there before?" Ryder said with a questioning glance.

Gabriella nodded. "Never. I'm sure that's not a popular trail so it might be overgrown. Hard to get up there and there is only one way up. He'll know I'm headed there."

"You can't surprise him," Diego said, worried that she'd be a sitting duck.

Gabriella pursed her lips and did a little shrug of delicate shoulders. "There might be another way. I can go up and around and come down from above him. I'd have the element of surprise that way."

"*We*, Gabriella. There's no way you're doing this alone," Ryder said, and quickly tacked on, "Along with a few other agents on the trail and with Diego."

Diego nodded and circled an area on the map that had snared his attention. "There are some man-made structures. Do you know of any other scout camp structures other than those we visited?"

Gabriella dipped her head, considering it, and then shook her head. "Not that I remember. But maybe Sophie and Robbie can find an older map of the camp?"

"I'll get them working on it. In the meantime, I'll start at the original camp and work my way to this area," Diego said, and trailed his finger along the monitor, showing the route Poppy and he would take.

"I'll arrange for other agents to meet us there as backup," Ryder said, and walked away to make the necessary calls and plans for the additional CBI agents.

"I've got a change of clothes in my trunk that are better suited for a hike. I can change once we're there," she said, and was about to walk away when he gently grasped her arm.

"You do not have to do this," he said, worried about what surprises the killer might have in store.

Her lips firmed into a thin slash, warning she wouldn't budge. Her next words confirmed it.

"I have to do this for me, but more importantly, those families deserve closure and those women deserve justice. Nothing else matters."

Chapter Twenty-Four

Jeannie Roberts huddled into a tight ball, fighting the shivers racking her body.

Cold, so cold, she thought.

A brisk wind whistled in through the gaps in the walls and swept up through the floorboards of the old shower stall.

She knew it was a shower stall from the rusty showerhead across from her.

That explained the gaps in the floorboards. They let water run off.

The other breaks in the wall were from where the wood had rotted out here and there, or shrunk from years of exposure.

He had tied her to one set of boards, and she'd tried for over an hour to break them, hoping that the weather had weakened them.

They'd given a little but held. If anything, it had made it harder for her since pulling them off the support beams had only created greater gaps that allowed the unseasonably cold spring air to stream through, chilling her.

She would die if she didn't get out of here soon.

The signs of hypothermia were already registering. The shivering and drowsiness. Slight confusion and cold on her skin.

She had to move. Stay alert. Giving in meant death.

She wasn't ready to die.

It took them well over half an hour to prep any materials they might need and make it to the old scout camp.

Another half an hour or more until the extra CBI agents arrived, including a sniper armed with an M40 rifle Diego recognized from his time in the Marines.

With all the agents gathered around, Gabriella laid out who would be going where on copies of the maps they had worked on earlier, which she passed out at their arrival.

"Diego will have Poppy search for Roberts along with you. We have identified this area as a possible killing field, so keep an eye out for anything unusual and mark it for our CSI team," she said, and pointed to two of the agents.

Running a finger along her map, she showed the remaining four agents their plan to flank Guarino. "We'll go up the trail together until we split up here. At that point, we should use extreme caution because we don't know what this killer has planned."

Gesturing to the sniper, she said, "Do you think you can get eyes on him from that area?"

The sniper looked at the map, then peered up the mountain toward the summit. "It may be possible."

"Good. Once you have eyes on him, let us know so we can assess if we need to change our plan," she said, glanced around the team gathered there and nodded.

"Let's go," she said. The agents immediately went into action, following the instructions they'd been given.

He hesitated, hating the thought of Gabriella being in danger, then reminded himself that this was the life she'd chosen. He had to support that in any way he could.

Because of that, he buried his fear deep and gave Poppy the track command.

"*Such*," he said, and doubled down with the hand command as well.

Poppy immediately took off, nosing the ground in front of them.

She didn't pick up on any scent immediately, so Diego guided her onto the trail for the scout camp.

It didn't take long to reach the buildings they'd already searched.

He didn't expect Poppy to get a hit, but he let her nose around anyway. They were looking for any possible trail that might lead to the areas they'd identified on the map.

Sure enough, as they reached the farthermost shower stalls, close to the area from which Isabella had disappeared, there seemed to be a path away from the camp and up the mountain.

The path had not been used in a long time, but there was still enough of a break in the underbrush and trees for them to follow.

They had only gone along that trail for about one hundred yards when Poppy suddenly stopped cold and raised her head. Instead of continuing up the trail, she pulled him through thicker underbrush and trees for several yards before nosing in a mound of leaves, old pine needles and vines.

She scented the area and then sat to signal she smelled something.

"What is it?" asked one of the agents who had been following behind him.

As he carefully examined the mound, he realized what it was.

"A grave," he said, and as sad as he was, he was also grateful.

Someone would be going home soon.

GABRIELLA GLANCED UP the trail.

No sign of Guarino, which was good.

If they couldn't see the killer, he probably couldn't see them. That was essential for being able to surprise and apprehend him.

The spot she'd picked for them to break apart was hopefully not a place where Guarino might detect their approach.

The doorbell chime of her phone erupted, shockingly loud against the silence of the mountain.

She whipped her phone out and silenced the sound.

Another message from that same unidentified number.

Another video, different from the first, of Roberts struggling to break free. The words in bloodred across this video said, "Time's running out."

She didn't need him to tell her that.

But worse, he was watching Roberts. If Diego found her before they did, Guarino might bolt from his location.

She texted a warning to Diego not to enter the building when they located Roberts.

A when and not an if. She had total faith in Diego and Poppy.

Once Diego acknowledged her warning, they proceeded up the trail, mindful that Guarino might also have trail cams to warn of their approach.

Luckily there was nothing, so they proceeded to the spot she had designated for them to separate.

She faced Ryder, wanting to be sure he was in support of this plan, and at his nod, she faced the sniper and another agent and said, "Hold here until we advise that we're in position to apprehend Guarino."

"Copy that," the two agents confirmed.

She was about to head up the trail when Ryder swept his arm out to stop her. "It's pretty overgrown," he said, and pulled out a small machete from a knapsack he'd brought with him.

"Okay, but we need to be careful. Sound travels far on mountainsides like this," she said, and as if to support her, Poppy's bark drifted up from below.

"Got it," he said, and carefully moved along the trail, both cutting and shoving aside brush to clear their way.

DIEGO HAD HOPED to reach the areas identified on the map much more quickly. Definitely before Gabriella and her team reached the summit and had a possible confrontation with the killer.

But along the way, Poppy had pulled him away from the trail

and to suspect areas multiple times. They had identified at least four other mounds that were possible grave sites and marked them for the CSI team.

Eventually, they returned to the trail and were halfway to Roberts's possible location when the sudden snap of a branch was followed by a shout of pain.

He whirled to find one of the agents had been speared in the leg by a booby trap.

Muttering a curse, he stopped the man as he tried to pull it out.

"Leave it in. We don't know if it's hit anything important," he said, afraid that if it had hit a large vessel, the agent would bleed out before they could get him back down the trail.

Facing the uninjured agent, he said, "Call for an ambulance and help him back down. Carefully."

"Got it," the man said, helped the injured agent to his feet and together they hobbled down to the trailhead.

Using the communications equipment they'd donned before heading up the trail, he called Gabriella.

"We've got a problem," he said.

Chapter Twenty-Five

Gabriella listened as Diego explained about the booby trap and ahead of her, Ryder paused, likewise hearing the conversation.

"How bad was he injured?" she asked, worried about her fellow agent.

"I don't think it was life-threatening, but we need to be alert," he said.

"Roger that. Be careful," she whispered, worried that Diego was heading to the other location on his own.

Ryder faced her, worry etched on his features. "Do you think he could have booby-trapped this trail?"

Uneasily, she shook her head. "I'm not sure. He thinks he can outsmart us and maybe he has. For now. We need to have eyes on every inch of ground."

He nodded. "Got it," he said, and this time, moved along the trail more slowly, vigilant for signs of any traps or snares.

It delayed them, way too much, much as it had delayed Diego, Gabriella worried.

With the wind on the mountain and unseasonable cold, Roberts had to quickly be losing body temperature. It could already be at fatally low levels.

As they broke free of the tree line above the location Guarino had pinned, it struck her that it was an absolutely glorious spring day.

No one should die on a day like today, she thought as they pushed ahead and reached the peak above Guarino's position.

Sure enough, he was exactly where he said he'd be, sitting on the ground in a lotus position, eyes closed as if he were in deep meditation. His hands rested peacefully on his knees but as she looked more closely, she noticed something in one hand.

Her gut tightened and in a whisper, she reached out to the sniper positioned below them.

"Do you have eyes on him?"

"I got him," the agent confirmed.

"What does he have in his right hand?" she asked.

What seemed like a painfully long time passed before he said, "A cell phone."

Diego stopped short as he heard the chatter between Gabriella and the sniper.

A cell phone? To talk to them or for something else? Like a bomb maybe?

Rushing ahead while aware of the danger, he reached a series of rickety buildings that resembled those in the scout camp located lower on the mountainside.

Gingerly he picked his way around them and as he did so, a soul-wrenching cry stopped him cold.

He listened again, trying to pinpoint where it had come from, and seconds later, the rattle of wood boards guided him toward the backmost hut.

"*Such*," he said to Poppy. She immediately moved in the direction of the sound and laid down next to one of the dilapidated shower stalls.

Roberts was visible between the gaps in the wall, naked skin pale against the darker wood of the building.

"Jeannie," he called out softly, and a soft whimper answered him before the tips of her fingers, nails broken and bloody from trying to escape, slipped through the gaps in the wood.

"I'm with CBI, Jeannie. We're here to help," he said.

"Don't leave me," she cried, and frantically yanked at the wood boards.

"I won't. I won't, Jeannie, but you need to help me. Do you see anything inside that looks like a booby trap or bomb?" he asked as he worked his way around the shower stall, searching for signs of any kind of danger whether a booby trap or bomb.

He had thought about training Poppy for explosives once but hadn't done it. Now he regretted it.

There were no visible signs of any booby traps or IEDs.

He approached the door of the stall, ready to open it, but as he did, a ray of sunlight, almost like a message from the heavens, illuminated the latch.

He saw it then.

A black wire, running from the latch and down to the ground.

He splayed on the ground and peered beneath the floor of the shower stall.

The wire from the latch connected to a black box a little bigger than a shoebox.

"Gabriella, I see what looks like a bomb. Opening the door will trip it," he advised, and then hopped to his feet.

"We need to defuse the situation and that bomb, Diego. Stay back," she said.

Gabriella took a step toward Guarino to speak to him, but Ryder grabbed hold of her arm to keep her back.

"What do you think you're doing?" he said in an urgent whisper.

"He said 'trade.' That can't happen if he doesn't see me," she said.

"It's too dangerous. We don't know if he hasn't booby-trapped himself as well," Ryder said, and peered down the slope, scrutinizing Guarino as he calmly sat there.

As if sensing his perusal, Guarino's eyes slowly drifted open, and a cruel smile slipped onto his lips.

He lifted the hand that held the cell phone, finger poised on the screen, and called out, "I wanted a trade, Gabriella. It doesn't seem as if you understood what I meant."

"Don't, Raul. Please," she said, and slowly approached him, hands help up in apology and to ask him to stop.

"Don't? Please? Is that all you have, Gabriella?" he said with a harsh laugh.

"What I have is enough evidence to put you away for a long time, Raul. Hard time unless you cooperate," Gabriella warned and continued her approach.

"Cooperate. I hate cooperation," he said with another, almost exasperated laugh. "You know what I did with women who tried to cooperate to get free?"

She didn't want to know, but the longer she kept him talking, the higher the possibility that Diego might be able to free Roberts.

"Why don't you tell me what you did? I bet you'd like to relive that," she said, and finally moved within several feet of him. That let her see the almost manic look in his gaze. A look that said that not all of them would leave this mountainside alive.

"I killed them slowly. Inch by inch you might say. A finger. A toe. Not the eyes, though. I wanted them to see what I was doing," he said gleefully.

"What about the others? The ones who fought back?" she asked, just to keep him talking.

"Ah, they were the best. It's why I keep them longer. A gift for their spirit," he said with a wistful smile.

"Is that why you kept Isabella?" she asked, preparing herself for his answer.

Guarino tsked and shook his head. "My little Isabella. She was my first, you know."

"I know. Why? Why did you take her?" she asked.

"She was so pretty. She would have been as beautiful as you

if I hadn't…" He stopped then, as if surprised by what he had planned to say next but then continued.

"I didn't mean to kill her," he said, his gaze pleading, as if seeking forgiveness.

But then darkness slipped into that gaze, as if another person was taking control.

"But I liked it. A lot. I knew it was wrong. I tried for a long time not to do it again, but it was too hard to fight the need," he admitted, and again, forgiveness and darkness twisted into a sick singsong in his tone.

"We can help you understand that need, Raul. There are therapists—"

"My father sent me to therapists! They know nothing," he screamed and wildly waved the hand with the cell phone.

She pumped her hands in the air, trying to urge calm, and once again said, "Please, Raul."

IT WAS A race against time, and Diego didn't intend to lose the race.

With one last swing around the shower stall to make sure there weren't other traps or bombs besides the one at the door, he examined the various slats.

Cheap, untreated pine that had suffered after years of exposure.

One wall seemed to have received the brunt of the exposure.

He found a larger gap where he could slip his finger in to grasp the side of the panel. Putting all his strength and weight into it, he yanked, trying to pull it free.

It snapped, sending him flying backward onto the ground.

He tossed aside the rotten slat and returned to the wall, breaking off another piece of wall and then another.

Bending, he looked inside to where Roberts was curled into a fetal position at the far side of the shower stall.

"I'm here, Jeannie. I'll have you out in a second."

Jerking against another slat, he snapped it and tossed it aside. Repeated it with yet another slat, creating enough space for him to slip through.

He jerked off his knapsack, tossed it away and gave Poppy a command to sit.

Bending, he eased through the gap and over to Roberts, who was barely conscious. He touched her arm. Her skin was ice-cold.

Too cold, he worried.

He ripped off his jacket and wrapped it around her.

She stirred then and opened her eyes, her gaze slightly unfocused first, and then fearful.

"I'm here to help, Jeannie. I'm with CBI," he repeated since it was clear that hypothermia was making her confused.

He pulled out a knife to cut the zip ties at her ankles and wrists, and she cried out "No" and kicked out at him.

"I'm with the police. I'm here to help," he said again, and it seemed as if it finally registered.

She stilled and he slipped the knife beneath the zip ties, cut them off and said, "Can you walk?"

"Maybe," she said hesitantly.

He nodded, eased an arm around her waist and helped her rise. Together they hobbled over to the hole he'd made in the wall.

Easing through the gap first, he then helped her exit, but she stumbled badly, falling into his arms.

"We have to move away from here, Jeannie," he said, bent and hauled her into his arms.

"Please put that down," Gabriella said with hands upraised, urging Guarino yet again to calm down.

"Please! You disappoint me, Gabriella. You deserve to suffer like the others," he said, his face almost purple with rage.

"We have to take him out, Gabriella," Ryder said across her earpiece.

She shook her head, and whispered back, "No. Hold your fire."

"You're suffering, just in a different way, Raul. You didn't want to hurt them. You just can't control yourself," she said, and took a step closer, hoping to grab the cell phone before he could trigger the bomb Diego had found.

A bomb that might kill Roberts as well as Diego and Poppy if they were still there with her.

"I don't need to control myself. I just need to control them. The women and you," he said, and calmed a little.

But that calm was more frightening than his earlier maniacal state.

He met her gaze, clear-eyed and determined. "I'm in control here, Gabriella. And I'm going to make you suffer," he said, and pressed his finger to the cell phone screen.

Chapter Twenty-Six

A blast of pressure pummeled him while sharp splinters pierced his back.

The force of the explosion sent him flying and as he fell, he protected Roberts and Poppy as best he could, hauling them beneath him as pieces of debris rained down.

Several of the pieces were on fire, and he bolted to his feet quickly to keep away from Roberts and Poppy, and to put them out before they could ignite a blaze.

On the ground, Roberts shivered despite his jacket. Poppy nosed around her, sensing her discomfort.

He called Poppy over, quickly examined her for injuries, and satisfied she was unharmed, he directed her to lie down beside Roberts. "*Platz*," he said, and once she had, he urged Roberts close to Poppy, hoping the warmth of the dog's body would help.

Then he went in search of his knapsack where he had an assortment of supplies, including survival blankets that would help.

The knapsack had been tossed several feet away and he grabbed it and rummaged through it to remove two survival blankets. Ripping open the bags, he wrapped Roberts in the blankets and massaged her legs and arms, trying to get warmth to return.

As he did that, he called out to the team. "Can anyone hear me?" he asked, and realized he could barely hear himself past the ringing in his ears caused by the blast and the dislodgment of his earpiece.

He jammed it back in place in time to hear the worried chatter across the line.

"Diego, copy. We hear you. Are you okay?" Gabriella asked.

"I am, but Roberts needs medical attention. I'm going to carry her down."

"Ambulance should already be there for the wounded agent," she said.

"What about Guarino?" he asked as he gently lifted Roberts into his arms, careful to keep the blankets and jackets tight around her to try and conserve what little body heat she had left.

"Dead. Sniper took him out after he triggered the bomb," she advised, and it was impossible to miss the frustration in her voice.

As he walked along the trail to the parking lot, he said, "It may not be the justice you wanted for Isabella, but...he can't hurt anyone ever again."

"No, he can't. But how will we ever get closure now for all those families and Isabella?" she asked, pain alive in her voice.

He hadn't wanted to tell her while they were trying to reach the summit, worried it would be a distraction. But there was no reason to delay any longer.

"We found possible burial sites. I marked them and can lead CSI back to the locations," he advised, stumbled on an exposed root he couldn't see because of his burden, and managed to catch himself before they went rolling down the trail.

Muttering a curse, he said, "I'll be waiting for you in the parking lot."

"Coming down as soon as I can," she said. He gave his attention to picking his way along the trail.

His arms and back ached from the weight of her, but she still hadn't roused enough to assist, and that worried him.

Had her body temperature dropped to fatal levels? he wondered and increased his pace as much as he could, Poppy loping just ahead of him. He was grateful to see that the dog seemed unaffected and unharmed by the explosion.

He lost track of time, plodding along, sweat running down his face and back from the exertion of carrying her.

With only yards to go, a pair of EMTs came running up the trail hauling a stretcher.

They quickly bundled Roberts onto the stretcher and hurried away with her, leaving him to trudge down the last little bit of the trail.

As he reached the parking lot, black circles danced in his vision, and his knees grew rubbery. He reached for a nearby tree trunk to steady himself and grasped it, the bark rough against his palm.

Focusing on that, he held on to consciousness. He wasn't ready to rest. Not until he'd led the CSI team to the five graves they'd found above the campgrounds.

As he sat there on the cold ground, another EMT walked over to him.

"Agent Rodriguez? Maybe we should take a look at you, too," he said, and offered a hand to help him to his feet.

He rose unsteadily, and Poppy was immediately at his side, giving him another anchor to reality.

Haltingly, he walked with the EMT to the back of a second ambulance that had answered their call for help. The EMT seated him there and immediately went to work, checking his vitals.

"Your blood pressure is a little low. We need to rehydrate you," he said, wrapped an emergency blanket around him and prepped an IV.

"Thanks," he said, and a second later, Poppy hopped up beside him. He wrapped an arm around her and checked her yet again for signs of any injury.

"You're okay, girl," he said.

"But you're not. We should go to the hospital to remove those splinters in your back," the EMT said.

"Can you take them out now?" he asked, not wanting to leave the area until he had led CSI to the graves and was there to help Gabriella if one of them was Isabella's.

The EMT lifted the blanket and examined his back. "Yes, but it'll hurt like a—"

"Do it," Diego asked, and met the EMT's dubious gaze. "Please. I'm not done here."

With an uneasy dip of his head, the EMT relented, got an IV into him and shifted the blanket so that he could pull out the splinters in his back.

The cold of scissors, cutting away his shirt, registered only seconds before a sharp pull sent pain radiating through his back. His muscles jumped and the EMT muttered, "Sorry, man. I'm trying to do it as painlessly as I can."

"It's fine," he mumbled behind his gritted teeth, and fought off the black circles again, closing his eyes to ignore them.

He had to stay strong. It wouldn't be the first time he'd been wounded and still had to work.

Burying his head against Poppy's soft fur, he focused on that to keep from jumping every time the fire erupted across his back.

"All are out. I'll just get them clean and bandaged, but when was the last time you had a tetanus shot?" the EMT said, his touch gentle as he swabbed disinfectant across the assorted wounds.

Diego flinched and said, "I'm up to date on shots."

The sound of sirens and crunch of gravel dragged his attention to the second ambulance that was pulling out of the parking lot.

"How is she doing?" he asked the EMT who had worked on him.

"Core body temperature was only eighty-two, so she had severe hypothermia. She's lucky you found her when you did," the EMT said, and offered Diego a sweatshirt from a cubby in the ambulance.

"It's a spare I keep. They said to give you this back," he said and handed him the jacket he had wrapped around Roberts.

Diego pulled on the sweatshirt and after, his jacket, which he'd have to toss after today. Feathery white down poked from several large tears, and blood marred various spots.

He jerked his arm through one sleeve and then stopped as he realized the IV was still in his other arm.

"Can you take that out?" he asked, and earned an eye roll from the EMT.

"It's against medical advice, but I know you won't listen anyway," he said, carefully extracted the IV and then quickly slapped an adhesive bandage to stop any bleeding.

GABRIELLA HIT THE ground of the parking lot almost at a run.

She stopped short as she caught sight of Diego with the EMT, Poppy at his side.

Racing over, she wrapped her arms around him, uncaring of how unprofessional it might look.

"I was so worried," she said.

"I'm okay," he said, which earned a guffaw from the nearby EMT and a muttered, "No, he's not."

Gabriella released her hold, stepped back and examined him. Streaks of dirt and a little blood marred his handsome face. Bits of twigs and some leaves were tangled in the longer strands of his hair. Beneath the dirt and blood, his tanned face was paler than usual.

She brushed her hand through those locks to get rid of the debris and said, "We should get you to the hospital."

He vehemently shook his head. "Not until the CSI team is here and I take them around."

She knew better than to argue. "Stubborn."

"Says the pot," he kidded.

"How is Roberts? CBI Agent Blake?" she asked, and looked around for another ambulance just as Ryder and the other agents came to join them.

"Roberts was suffering from extreme hypothermia. The agent was lucky that the stake didn't hit anything important. Both are on their way to the hospital," the EMT advised as he worked to clean up his rig.

"I'm going to send Agent McIntosh to the hospital to check on Roberts and Blake. Hopefully, we were able to get to Roberts in time," Ryder said, and scrutinized Diego.

"Looks like we should get you there also," he said.

"I'm good. Just a few cuts and scrapes," Diego replied, and slipped off the back of the ambulance to stand as if to prove he was truly fine. With a hand command, Poppy hopped down and heeled at his side.

The sound of a vehicle drew their attention to the entrance of the parking lot, where three CSI vans were pulling in along with a duo of vans from the medical examiner's office.

Ryder looked at them and said, "Do you want me to take one of the CSI teams to the summit where Agent Samuels is securing the scene, and you go with Diego to the graves?"

There was an unspoken question there also: Are you ready to possibly find your sister after so many years?

"Yes, please do that. I'll go with Diego, Poppy and the CSI team," she said, and slipped her hand into Diego's, needing that connection.

She'd always thought of herself as tough and independent, but when finally faced with knowing what had happened to Isabella, she suddenly didn't want to be so independent.

A gentle squeeze on her hand reassured her that he would be there for her.

In a flurry of activity, Diego was identifying on the map

what Poppy had confirmed with her searches while Ryder returned to the summit with one of the CSI teams.

As a final confirmation of Guarino's evil, they realized that the graves were arranged in the shape of a cross with one grave in the center of the formation.

"Do you think…" she began but couldn't finish, overwhelmed with emotion.

"I think the center grave, the heart of the cross, may be Isabella," he said, confirming what she had been thinking.

"Do you want us to start there, Agent Ruiz?" one of the CSI techs asked.

Gabriella shook her head. "Start where you think is the best place to preserve evidence. I won't let my connection possibly damage the case."

With a solemn nod, the agent faced Diego. "We're ready when you are."

DIEGO EXAMINED GABRIELLA'S face, trying to gauge if she had prepared herself for what the investigations might reveal.

Her face was all severe lines, and all life had left her normally warm and engaging gaze. She had her game face on, but from the trembling of her hand in his, it was clear she was struggling to hold it together.

But they had a job to do. Gabriella knew that more than most.

He nodded and said, "I'll lead you up to the killing fields."

With a soft click under his tongue to Poppy and a gentle tug on Gabriella's hand, he pushed off in the direction of the trailhead.

His legs felt slightly unsteady, as if he was on a ship at sea instead of on land, but he ignored that. Just like Gabriella had to stay strong, he had to as well. He could rest once those up on that mountainside finally found their peace.

He pushed on, carefully watching for exposed roots and anything else that might trip him up. He didn't think he could handle another fall. He already had enough aches blossoming all across his body.

It took nearly half an hour before they hit what might be the first grave and just to confirm that they hadn't been wrong, he once again instructed Poppy to search.

"*Such*," he said, and much as she had done earlier, Poppy nosed around the area and then lay down near the spot they had identified earlier.

The lead CSI agent directed one of his team to work on the first grave.

Diego and Poppy repeated the process for the other four graves.

Once they had done that, the CSI agents swarmed the area, beginning the work of gathering evidence and recovering Guarino's victims.

The lead agent stood before them and said, "I'm going to request more agents and lights since it'll be dark in another hour or so. But it's going to take time. Maybe you should return to Denver to wait. We'll let you know once we have anything."

Chapter Twenty-Seven

Gabriella had thought she was ready to know what had happened to Isabella.

But as she took note of all the activity at the scene and then peered at Diego, who was bravely standing there despite his injuries, she realized that it was time to step away and let others do what they did best.

She had already done all she could to get them here, as had Diego and Poppy.

"Let's go back to CPS and fill them in on what's happening," she said with a firm squeeze on Diego's hand.

His gaze skipped over her features. "Are you sure?"

"I am. We all need some rest and...separation from this," she said, and with a gentle tug on his hand, they hurried to her car.

As she drove, Diego called Sophie and Robbie with his report and after he ended the call, he said, "Do you mind if I just close my eyes for a moment?"

"No, go ahead," she said, but was worried that he was hurt far worse than he had let on.

She kept an eye on the road but did the same with Diego to make sure he was fine.

His soft even breaths said he slept, and as she tenderly touched his hand as it rested on his leg, the cold was gone, replaced by a warmth that lessened some of her worry.

He roused as she made the last turn off the highway and onto the street for the CPS offices.

"How are you feeling?" she said as she turned into the parking lot and then pulled into one of the spots reserved for CPS.

"Achy. Some pain on my back," he admitted, and blew out a tired sigh. "Why don't I feel satisfaction that Guarino is dead?"

"Because his victims and their families won't get justice?" she said, shut off the car and faced him.

With a shrug and toss of his hands, he said, "Some might think justice was served by the sniper, but I think the families might have wanted to know why. Right?"

He nailed her with his gaze because she was one of those families. "Does the why matter? Isabella is gone. Taken too soon, but hopefully she'll be home now."

Nodding, he cradled her cheek. "I know I'm sorry doesn't cut it, but I'm sorry."

She cupped his hand, stroked it and offered him a weak smile. "Thank you."

The beep of his phone shattered the moment. He glanced at it and said, "Sophie and Robbie. They have dinner waiting for us."

"That Robbie is a bottomless pit," she said with a chuckle, but deep down, she recognized it was their way of offering comfort at a difficult time. Her Mexican mother would have done the same.

She exited the car while Diego got out, unharnessed Poppy and grabbed his knapsack from the back.

"I'll have to feed her, too, while we eat and then walk her," he said as they strolled over to the elevator bank.

Since it was after normal business hours, the elevator arrived quickly and in no time they were in the Crooked Pass Security offices. The heavenly smells of food filled the space as they walked in, and Gabriella's stomach growled in response.

She covered her midsection with her hand as Diego smiled and said, "I'm starving, too. We never got lunch."

No, they hadn't, because too much had been happening too quickly.

But no longer. Now it was time to sit and wait for the CSI experts to do their work.

Sophie rushed from the conference room, concern etched on her features.

"Are you okay?" she asked, and examined Diego from head to toe.

Diego pointed to a washroom at the end of the hall. "I'm going to clean up before we sit to eat," he said, and didn't wait for a reply to walk off, Poppy obediently at his side.

Sophie peered at her and said, "I wish I could help more somehow."

Gabriella closed the distance between them and hugged the other woman. "Sophie, if it wasn't for you, Robbie and the rest of your team, I don't think we would have saved Jeannie Roberts and found the others."

Sophie tightened the embrace and said, "I wish we could have helped more."

"You've done what seemed impossible," Gabriella said, grateful for all their help.

Robbie popped out of the conference room and took in the scene. She waited for his usual quips, but he only offered a sad smile and went back in.

Sophie and she followed him and when Diego entered, they sat and ate, fairly silent as hunger and the realization that the case was almost done hung over them.

When they finished, Diego fed Poppy her kibble although he had been sneaking her tidbits from the Cuban food that the siblings had ordered from Diego's favorite restaurant.

"I've got to take her for a walk," he said once Poppy had gobbled down her food.

"I'll go with you," she said. They went to street level, strolling in silence for a few blocks, letting the German shepherd relieve herself and get some air before returning to the office.

As Diego turned at one point, she noticed the damage to the

jacket and realized that each tear and bloodstain on the fabric meant he was wounded beneath them.

She gently stroked her hand across his back and said, "Are you sure you don't need to go to the hospital?"

He waved her off. "I'm okay. The EMT took care of it."

Since he wasn't going to give in at that moment, she let it go, although she intended to press him later and tend to the injuries.

As they returned to the conference room, Ryder was sitting there, eating some food that Sophie had set aside for him.

He smiled stiffly, worrying her.

"How was it going at the scout camp?" she asked.

"Good, but it's going to take time. CSI agent said he'll update us in the morning," Ryder said.

She'd been waiting nearly eight years to find Isabella. Several more hours wasn't going to make a difference, and the time away from the case might let her prepare for finally finding her sister.

"That sounds good," she said, earning a raised eyebrow from Ryder, as if he didn't believe she was giving in so quickly.

"Time to go then. Selene is waiting for me," Robbie said, and rose.

"We'll meet back here at nine," Sophie said, and ran a loving hand across Ryder's shoulders.

"Nine. That's good," Gabriella said, and glanced at Diego, who nodded.

"I'm good with that. I'll walk you to your car."

It sounded to her like he'd be going his own way tonight, which roused disappointment. Even though she no longer needed his protection with Guarino gone, she'd hoped for...

What had you hoped for? the little voice in her head challenged. *Love in just a few days?*

Surprisingly, that's just what she felt for him in an incredibly short time.

When they reached her car, she stopped and faced him. "I

want to thank you for all that you, Poppy and the team have done," she said, and rubbed Poppy's head, earning an appreciative lick of her hand.

"She likes you," Diego said with a happy laugh, and then his gaze locked with hers. "I like you, too. A lot."

Relief flooded through her, and she smiled. "The feeling is mutual. Actually, it's more than just like, Diego. Ridiculous as it sounds, I love you."

A rough breath escaped him, and a broad grin erupted on his face. He cradled her cheek, stepped closer and whispered against her lips, "I love you, too, Gabriella."

"I hope that means you'll come home with me tonight. I don't want to be alone," she said.

GOING HOME WITH GABRIELLA. It had been so long since he'd felt that he had a home, but that's how he felt with her. As if he was finally where he belonged.

"Let's go home," he said, and in a rush, they packed Poppy into the car and were on their way to her home.

When they entered and got Poppy settled for the night, Gabriella said, "Let's take a look at your back, and I won't take no for an answer."

"Yes, ma'am," Diego said with a little salute, aware she wouldn't give up.

She grabbed his hand and led him to her en suite bathroom where he sat on the toilet, his back to her.

He jerked off his shirt, biting back a groan at the pain that erupted across his back from the movement. But then her gentle touch drifted across his skin, offering comfort.

Comfort he hadn't felt in so long with anyone else.

Quickly and efficiently, she applied more antibiotic ointment on the wounds and fresh bandages. As he stood and faced her, she offered him some over-the-counter painkillers.

"I wish I had something stronger," she said.

He shook his head. "These are fine. I want to keep sharp," he said, but not because he was worried about an attack. Instead, it was because he didn't want to miss a minute of being with her.

She nodded, slipped her hand into his and led him toward her bed, stopping at the edge.

Turning, she faced him, her gaze questioning. "Are we foolish to feel like this?"

He shook his head. "Foolish is never being able to feel like this. I know that because for too long I couldn't feel anything."

Smiling, she splayed a hand over his heart. "I want to feel everything with you," she said, freeing the last of his restraint.

They rushed to bed, clothes tossed in their haste to be together. As he joined with her, it was like coming home after being lost in the desert for far too long. They moved together, seeking release but also completion of a different kind.

As they finally fell over together, he cuddled her close and said again, "I love you."

She stroked a hand across his chest and kissed the underside of his jaw. "I love you, too," she said, and pillowed her head on his chest.

He held her close, offering her comfort in the aftermath of their loving. She'd need that and more in the morning, he suspected.

He didn't doubt that one of the graves was Isabella's. Probably the one in the center, as if she was the heart of Guarino's hideous crimes.

It was with those thoughts skipping through his brain that he drifted off to an uneasy sleep that seemed too short when the first rays of sunlight drifted in through the French doors of her bedroom.

They had just finished showering when Gabriella's cell phone rang.

She answered, and her body stiffened instantly. With curt replies, she answered whoever was on the other end of the line.

"Yes, I get it. I'll be there," she said, and ended the call.

GABRIELLA FACED DIEGO, who stood there with question in his gaze. "That was the lead CSI agent. They've removed one of the victims to the ME's office and want me to come in for a possible identification."

"Isabella?" he said, dark brows rising in emphasis.

"They believe so from what they have. I mean, it's not possible to ID her face, but...we should go," she said, unable to voice what she'd see when she got to the ME. Unable to process what would remain of her loving, inquisitive and amazing baby sister.

She took a step away, but he tenderly wrapped her in his embrace. "I'm here for you. For whatever," he said.

Choking back a sob, she said, "I know."

They hurriedly dressed, delaying only to feed Poppy and then let her relieve herself outside.

The German shepherd seemed to sense their haste since she gobbled the food quickly and wasted little time in the yard.

It wasn't a long drive to the ME's office, but it seemed interminable that morning.

As they parked and walked to the front door, she realized Sophie, Ryder and Robbie were there to offer support.

"I appreciate you being here," she said, and together they walked in. Once Gabriella and Ryder had checked in, one of the medical examiners came out from the back and led them to a waiting area for victims' families.

"This may be difficult, Agent Ruiz," the ME said, and nervously fingered a clipboard between his hands.

"I understand. What do you have?" she asked, trying to keep her voice as neutral and professional as possible.

"We have dental records from your sister's case. Also her medical records. You may not remember all the details from them—"

"Her wisdom teeth were impacted, and she had them removed. She also had one slightly crooked front tooth. Her central incisor," she said and pointed out that tooth in her mouth before continuing. "She'd fallen off her bike the summer before and broke her arm. Her radius about midway," she said, and once again demonstrated it on her body.

The ME nodded. "That's consistent with what we have in our records, and also with the victim we removed from the central grave at the location. I'm so sorry, Agent Ruiz."

"I want to see her," Gabriella said with purpose.

"Agent Ruiz, this will be difficult—"

"I want to see her," she repeated, her tone leaving no doubt that she wouldn't waver from that request.

With another nod, the ME held the clipboard out in the direction of the door.

Diego laid his hand on her back, offering comfort and support as she stepped into the hallway and then followed the ME as he walked to the morgue door.

He opened the door, and they stepped inside. Three tables had sheets draped over their occupants.

He walked her to one and slowly pulled away the sheet to reveal a skeleton that had been reassembled on the shiny steel table.

"We don't have all of Isabella as the grave was subject to some scavenging—" he began, but Gabriella raised a hand to stop him.

She was well familiar with what happened to bodies buried in areas frequented by animals. She didn't want to imagine that with her sister.

And it was Isabella. She did not doubt that.

The dental and medical details were there for her to see. As was her general height.

Diego squeezed her shoulder, offering reassurance, and she nodded, shakily said, "Thank you. I appreciate all that you're doing."

With that, they left the morgue and rejoined the CPS team in the waiting room.

Sorrow filled her, but so did something else. Determination.

"This shouldn't have happened to Isabella. But it also shouldn't have happened to those other women. We had evidence that might have helped. They shouldn't have been cold cases for so long," she said as she recalled the finding that there had been touch DNA on one of the victims that hadn't been found during the first investigation.

Ryder nodded in agreement. "We can do more. Working with Crooked Pass Security has proved that," he said, and glanced at Sophie and Robbie.

"We're in," Robbie said without hesitation.

"Good. These aren't going to be the only cold cases we solve," she said, and together, they all walked back to their cars, but as they neared hers, she faced Diego.

"I want you to be a part of more than just what Crooked Pass Security does, Diego. I want you to be a part of my life," she said, cupped his cheek and ran her thumb across his lips.

His smile beneath her thumb registered a second before he said, "I want to be a part of your life, Gabriella. I love you."

She went on tiptoes to kiss him and wrapped her arms around his waist, mindful of his injuries.

He enveloped her in his embrace and at his side, Poppy barked and hopped happily.

She laughed and bent to rub the dog's head, earning several doggy kisses as she said, "I want you, too, Poppy."

Her phone chirped to warn of a message, and she glanced at it.

The lead CSI agent wanted them back at the scout camp.

She showed it to Diego, and he nodded. "I'm ready whenever you are."

She slipped her hand into his and said, "I'm ready. For everything."

* * * * *

Get up to 4 Free Books!

**We'll send you 2 free books from each series you try
PLUS a free Mystery Gift.**

FREE Value Over **$25**

Both the **Harlequin Intrigue®** and **Harlequin® Romantic Suspense** series feature compelling novels filled with heart-racing action-packed romance that will keep you on the edge of your seat.

YES! Please send me 2 FREE novels from the Harlequin Intrigue or Harlequin Romantic Suspense series and my FREE gift (gift is worth about $10 retail). After receiving them, if I don't wish to receive any more books, I can return the shipping statement marked "cancel." If I don't cancel, I will receive 6 brand-new Harlequin Intrigue Larger-Print books every month and be billed just $7.19 each in the U.S. or $7.99 each in Canada, or 4 brand-new Harlequin Romantic Suspense books every month and be billed just $6.39 each in the U.S. or $7.19 each in Canada, a savings of 20% off the cover price. It's quite a bargain! Shipping and handling is just 50¢ per book in the U.S. and $1.25 per book in Canada.* I understand that accepting the 2 free books and gift places me under no obligation to buy anything. I can always return a shipment and cancel at any time by calling the number below. The free books and gift are mine to keep no matter what I decide.

Choose one: ☐ **Harlequin Intrigue Larger-Print** (199/399 BPA G36Y)   ☐ **Harlequin Romantic Suspense** (240/340 BPA G36Y)   ☐ **Or Try Both!** (199/399 & 240/340 BPA G36Z)

Name (please print)

Address   Apt. #

City   State/Province   Zip/Postal Code

Email: Please check this box ☐ if you would like to receive newsletters and promotional emails from Harlequin Enterprises ULC and its affiliates. You can unsubscribe anytime.

Mail to the Harlequin Reader Service:
IN U.S.A.: P.O. Box 1341, Buffalo, NY 14240-8531
IN CANADA: P.O. Box 603, Fort Erie, Ontario L2A 5X3

Want to explore our other series or interested in ebooks? Visit www.ReaderService.com or call 1-800-873-8635.

---

*Terms and prices subject to change without notice. Prices do not include sales taxes, which will be charged (if applicable) based on your state or country of residence. Canadian residents will be charged applicable taxes. Offer not valid in Quebec. This offer is limited to one order per household. Books received may not be as shown. Not valid for current subscribers to the Harlequin Intrigue or Harlequin Romantic Suspense series. All orders subject to approval. Credit or debit balances in a customer's account(s) may be offset by any other outstanding balance owed by or to the customer. Please allow 4 to 6 weeks for delivery. Offer available while quantities last.

Your Privacy—Your information is being collected by Harlequin Enterprises ULC, operating as Harlequin Reader Service. For a complete summary of the information we collect, how we use this information and to whom it is disclosed, please visit our privacy notice located at https://corporate.harlequin.com/privacy-notice. Notice to California Residents – Under California law, you have specific rights to control and access your data. For more information on these rights and how to exercise them, visit https://corporate.harlequin.com/california-privacy. For additional information for residents of other U.S. states that provide their residents with certain rights with respect to personal data, visit https://corporate.harlequin.com/other-state-residents-privacy-rights/.